June 16
2000

The
Storyteller's Goddess

The *Storyteller's Goddess*

Tales of the Goddess and
Her Wisdom from Around the World

Second Edition—Revised and Expanded

Carolyn McVickar Edwards

Illustrations by Kathleen Edwards

Marlowe & Company • New York

Published by
Marlowe & Company
841 Broadway, 4th Floor
New York, NY 10003

The Storyteller's Goddess: Tales of the Goddess and Her Wisdom from Around the World.
Second Edition.

Library of Congress Cataloging-in-Publication Data

    Edwards, Carolyn McVickar.
       The storyteller's goddess : tales of the goddess and her wisdom from around the world/
    by Carolyn McVickar Edwards.
       p. cm.
    Originally published: San Francisco : HarperSanFrancisco, © 1991.
    Includes bibliographical references.
    ISBN 1-56924-648-3
    1. Goddesses. I. Title.

BL473.5 .E38 2000
291.2'114—dc21   99-045011

0 9 8 7 6 5 4 3 2 1

Book design by Kathleen Lake, Neuwirth and Associates

Printed in the United States of America
Distributed by Publishers Group West

Contents

Contents

Contents

Acknowledgments

S tories about the goddess?" asks a man at a party. "Is that like about
men getting their heads cut off?"

No.

I look at his ordinary, well-meaning face. His mouth is not earnest,
but he isn't altogether joking.

My mouth opens and closes, words coming out, trying to make an
incisive connection for this person, reeling from the enormity of the
territory we could cover.

We could start with her stories. Just plunge in, not with the myriad
facts about the female deity in her countless forms, nor even with an
explanation of this earth-centered world view that is radical in its uni-
fication of things and ideas our culture (and this nice man) imagine to
be diametrically opposed.

The stories are her voices, her faces, her thighs.

This book is a collection of them, largely from the inspirations of

Merlin Stone's *Ancient Mirrors of Womanhood* and Janet McCrickard's *Eclipse of the Sun*. Some stories came whole for retelling; others I bent to what I believe are current sensibilities; some I formed from shards of image and concept. The tales comprise some thirty-nine understandings of goddess from some twenty-seven cultures. This new edition has six new stories, and many of the original stories have been reworked. Each one is accompanied by an introduction setting it in cultural, historical, and personal context.

Read them aloud. Tell them to the children. Sing them at the turnings of the year. Seed the loving heresies: death and dark are as much a part of the great cycle as life and light; body and mind are one; sister earth and all her stuffs and creatures are holy.

Thank you to Barbara Moulton for her original vision and to Patrice Wynne and Matthew Lore for carrying it on.

Introduction

Seven Goddess Principles—Truths Inside of Truths

Once, when I was a little girl, I played for an afternoon with a set of Russian nesting dolls. I am wistful thinking of them: sturdy, round, kindly, rosy-cheeked, with painted shawls and smiles; all alike, except that none was the same size as another. Each parted at her ample waist in order that all the smaller dolls fit inside. I arranged their glossy little bodies, returning them to their sisters' bellies; counting them with all the dreamy keenness of a miser with her gold.

These seven goddess principles feel like those nesting dolls as I fondle their intricacies and imagine how they may fit together. The principles seem not hierarchical but concentric in relation to one another. The most flexible concept, that of the goddess's totality of light and dark, seems like the mama doll holding within her all the other concepts. Like the dolls, each principle can be examined separately, but each is fully itself when played with as part of a spiral of questions and felt truths.

I. **All in All: Healing the Split**
Goddess is both light and dark.

II. **Constant Change: The Everlasting Cycle**
Goddess is the endless circle of life and death.

III. **Spirit Incarnate: Goddess as Earth and Body**
Goddess is the stuff of the planet and our fleshly selves.

IV. **The Force of Life: Sexuality and Creativity**
Goddess is everlasting, burgeoning desire.

V. **Surrender**
Goddess loosens cities from foundations and flesh from bones.

VI. **Goddess as Archetype**
Goddess is the holy feminine of the individual and collective unconsciousnesses.

VII. **Recovery of Herstory**
Goddess has been worshipped by civilizations of people whose reverence for female and earth has been remarkably underreported, even deliberately erased. In reclaiming herstory, the stories of ourselves becomes whole.

My relationship with goddess in the nearly sixteen years since I began this book is based on simply giving her attention. I've begged the moon; I've bestowed jewels in the crotch of a gnarled tree; I've sung, costumed, dreamed, chanted, and drummed. Any archetype to which we give energy comes more alive. Even a goddess whose name has not been spoken for a thousand years wakes up when we call her aloud. To show itself, the divine wants merely our reciprocity. Here is the true meaning of the word religion—from the Latin *re,* meaning *again,* and *ligare,* meaning *to bind, bond, or bridge.* To bind ourselves to her, we build the bridge of our attention again and again.

The book's first edition found me passionate as a convert about a way of understanding the world diametrically opposed to the male-elevating, body-scorning, shadow-shafting Christian fundamentalism of my childhood. I had met the goddess; I was eating her; she was coming out my pores. I was talking to her four directions on my daily walks, making rituals with women, building altars, fitting pagan words to Christian hymns and carols, painting her, sculpting her. I was convinced I needed to dance her, too, then stymied by the stiffness of my grieving, well-behaved body.

It had been God, God, God. Now it would be Goddess, Goddess, Goddess. We had to change! Out of all these newly discovered pieces of ancient earth-worship, we had to make a new religion for ourselves! Our health and the planet's depended on it.

They say people teach what they need to learn. Certainly true for me. Today, my body more and more alive, I'm as likely to try to empty myself of all but breath as I am to conduct a ritual; to bend into yoga shapes as I am to talk to the four directions. The dozens of altars have altered me: I've convinced myself. Her images glow like organs inside me.

Lately, I'm aiming to return my yard to a semblance of the intricate crosshatching of life it must have been before the suburbs swallowed it. It's just dawning on me that plants are not mere decoration nor even simply oxygen-producing biomass. They are food and shelter for animals who, in turn, eat each other. The great goddess of love, fertility, and slaughter sleeps right here in the belly of my starved blip of real estate.

Creator, preserver, destroyer, goddess stands like an enormous Asian statue behind me, her little toe towering over my head. Playing in her shadow, I am deeper and softer than I was before I lived with her names and stories.

I

All in All

Healing the Split

We live in a culture accustomed to the mental act of splitting. We're consciously trained to understand the world in disconnected opposites: good and bad, light and dark, male and female, high and low, mind and body, heaven and hell, spirit and earth. Subconsciously we pursue these divisions within ourselves. We acknowledge only the "acceptable," hiding away what the culture deems shameful or fearsome; and then—since the balance will insist upon itself—projecting our own so-called "ickinesses" onto Other.

Perhaps our deepest soul need is to have a relationship with the outside wholenesses that mirrors our inside wholenesses. The conscious work becomes the owning of our habits of splittage and the purposeful embrace of all the parts.

The divine as goddess encourages this work. She is the all in all. Unlike the still pervasive western understandings of the divine, in which good is split from bad and male from female, understanding her obliges us to synthesize the opposites. This is perhaps the most profound of all the commitments in goddess thinking. It's a thinking that feels; a body that speaks; a seeing that rests blind; a fullness of perception empty of certainty. It's a deliberate embrace of paradox as a match to the experience of self and world.

Goddess defies dissection and definition. She is earth and sky, water, fire, and metal. She is the word and the silence. She is body-mind, dark-light, wet-dry, down-up. She wraps herself around the boundaries of mature adulthood which requires us to operate out of coexisting contradictions. She is the we and the other. She is all the parts, the polarities of our souls, our neighbors, our strangers. She is the earthquake, the divorce, the firing; the burgeoning, the marriage, the deepening.

We are she and simultaneously her children and worshippers. She is the ebb and the flow; her tides pour through us. Bast, the cat goddess of ancient Egypt, sleek, dignified, mysterious, and affectionate, also tortures her prey. In this goddess view of the world with its conjunction of opposites, can we understand a morality?

Yes. It's a morality based on neither rules nor separations, but on relationship. The goddess view assumes a web of interactions in which nothing is disconnected. It assumes that all that is spent simply takes another form; that we live with the all, even when our minds are tempted to split our actions from their effects.

If I am unsure of right action, the rule is simple: all that I do comes back to me three times. Goddess morality expects me to struggle with the affirmation of my dreams and hopes in the context of the whole range of my feelings, and in clear sight of my responsibilities and circumstances. My productions and consumptions reverberate; simple living, composting, and recycling become rites; respect for earth and the creatures becomes reverence.

Pele, Volcano Woman

(PAY-lay)
Hawaii

Introduction

Pele is the goddess who lives in Mount Kilauea on the Hawaiian Islands. Goddess of fire in the earth, she is queen of the wonder and terror evoked by the still current and lethally beautiful phenomenon of the earth's turning inside out. A visitor to Mount Kilauea today may pay a tidy sum for a helicopter ride over her steaming mouth.

Early nineteenth-century missionaries encouraged Pele's people's simultaneous conversion to Christianity and her desecration through such methods as throwing stones of defiance into her crater. As late as the 1950s, however, some Hawaiians still knew the chants and gifts that would please her and petition her mercy. During more than one volcanic eruption in that period, proper supplication preceded the cessation of lava at the edge of several villages.

Mythology has it that the Hawaiian hula began when Pele asked her sisters to express delight through dance. To this day the hula, danced by Hawaiians in the ongoing process of retrieving ancient ways secularized by Christianity and the tourist industry, almost always includes move-

5

ment sacred to Pele. Powerful chants honor the history of her wrath, impatience, violence, and force in shaping the land. Jealousy and revenge are major themes in Pele's story cycle today, as are the magical potency of music and chanted song in love and romance. From Pele's stories, hula dancers today derive chants for dance preparation and conversations between lovers or family members. Then—ankles, necks, and foreheads ringed with ferns—they recreate the movements that have doubtless honored the spirits of earth, fire, water, and air since time out of mind.

In writing Pele's story, I struggled with how to convey the simultaneous accessibility of Pele as goddess woman and her terrible, murderous mystery. My pleas for inspiration to Volcano Woman as I walked and chanted her name early one Sunday morning were answered in a conversation with the proprietor of the corner store where I had stopped to buy milk. From a small village in India, he told me, his family still worshipped five elements: fire, water, air, earth, and metal. And the deity, he said, was the "great balancer of life and death." With this luminous phrase, the how-and-why love tale of Pele was set suddenly like a jewel in a ring, and I went home to write.

Pele's stone is obsidian and her colors are red and black. Pele helps me to accept the force of my own feelings and live with questions about natural tragedy.

The Romance of Volcano and Ocean

hen the center of the earth swells red hot and roars to meet the sky and rivers of fire race down the mountain, the people cry in terror. Even the old ones who know the name of Volcano Woman bring her presents of silk and tobacco with their knees trembling. At the edge of her mouth they set their gifts, and though her steaming cry does not sound like she is grateful, more than once her liquid fire has stopped at the edge of the village and the people and their animals are left alive.

Pele is the name of Volcano Woman, and no one really knows why she comes from the center of the earth dressed in her terrible beauty. Some people say it is not really Pele that comes from the center, but her children instead. Long ago, they say, when Pele was young, the center of the earth glowed with her loveliness. Her skin was black as coal and her

7

hair red as flames. Singing her song that hissed like steam through a small opening, she was content for a million years to putter in her house, stirring her red pepper soup in her huge iron pot. Sometimes she would sleep for a hundred years at a time, her arms wrapped around her brown and yellow snakes.

Then one day, Pele walked to the edge of the center and pushed her hands upward. That was the day Pele met Ocean. For in pushing upward, Pele made a crack in the center, and through the crack came Ocean's voice, deep and soft.

"Pele, may I come in?" asked Ocean.

Pele drew back. "I don't know you," she said.

"Then let us meet here again and again and talk until we do know each other," said Ocean.

That was how the conversations began. For a thousand years, Pele came to the crack and talked with Ocean. Some days Ocean didn't answer her call. But she could hear his voice boiling and dark in the distance. And some days Pele didn't come at Ocean's call. But every day they did talk, Pele's heart swelled with curiosity and wonder. For Ocean asked her about her soup and her snakes. He asked her what she dreamed when she slept. He asked her about the shapes of her rocks. Ocean told her about his wet purple world. He told her about the color green, and he told her about the sky.

One day, Pele whispered to Ocean that she loved him.

"Oh, my Pele," said Ocean. My wonderful friend," said Ocean. "Will you let me come in now?"

Pele felt her skin prickle. "Ocean, I am afraid," she said.

But she curled her fingers into the edges of the crack and pulled. Her muscles rippled and the crack opened wide. Ocean fell into her arms.

That was the beginning, the people say, of the marriage of Pele and Ocean. Some say it is when Pele is fighting with her husband that the volcano bursts. Others say that lava is the offspring of Pele and Ocean. It is the fire of Pele that makes the lava red hot, and the water of Ocean that makes it flow like a mighty river.

But some of the old ones shake their heads. No one knows the Volcano Woman, they say—not even Ocean. The volcano explodes only when Pele comes up from the center to balance the great scale of life and death. The volcano woman is the great balancer, they say.

But that is another story.

Amaterasu Omikami,
She Who Possesses Noon

(ah–mah–ter–RAH–su   oh–mee–KAH–mee)

Japan

Introduction

The eight-armed mirror of the sun goddess Amaterasu Omikami can be seen to this day in the Shinto shrine near the town of Uji Yamada by the Ise River in Japan. The Shinto religion, widespread in Japan today, is a synthesis of deep nature reverence and the political belief that Japan's royal family derives its heritage from the divine ancestress herself, Amaterasu Omikami. Perhaps the eight arms of the mirror are reminiscent of a sea creature like the octopus that ancients may once have imagined to hold up their many-islanded world. Speculate we can; ascertain we cannot, for written records of Amaterasu's story begin in the eighth century of this Common Era, along with all the other records of ancient Japan. The *Kojiki* and the *Nihongi,* commissioned in 712 C.E.,★ provide keys to understanding Japanese mythology. While both honor Amaterasu as a major deity, accounts of her origin differ (in

---

★The abbreviation C.E. stands for "Common Era," equivalent to the use of A.D. "Before the Common Era" is denoted by the letters B.C.E., equivalent to the use of B.C.

much the same way that biblical gospel accounts of the life of Jesus vary), and the texts show clear patriarchal biases as well. We also know that eighth-century scribes intentionally synthesized two bodies of belief and imagery: Buddhist and Shinto. In both texts, however, Amaterasu speaks of Izanami as her mother. The ancient Izanami may well have been a great serpent of the sea, responsible for the formation of land and life. (See story of Nu Kua.) Her daughter, Amaterasu, the sun, was born from her eye.

Amaterasu's story is my version of the myth of the sun goddess and her brother Susanowo (sue-sah-NO-woe), the ocean, told in Merlin Stone's *Ancient Mirrors of Womanhood*. The myth perhaps reenacts the tenuous nature of the annual rice-growing cycle on an island world at the mercy of the sea. Then, too, the winter solstice of every year parallels the time when Amaterasu Omikami shuts herself away in her cave. The tree beside the Ise River shrine is hung, to this day, with jewels and mirrors to attract her returning light.

The *kami* of Amaterasu's second name, Omikami, is defined as spiritual essence. Shinto worshippers honor the living *kami* in each part of the natural environment. Though the word *omi* in Japanese has no particular meaning, its similarity to the prefix *omni*, meaning *all*, helps me to understand her all-inclusivity.

Amaterasu Omikami's symbol is the mirror. I call on her at winter solstice and at times when a quality, attitude, or project nurtured in the cave of myself needs to emerge.

Japan's is one of several cultures whose peoples know, or have known, the sun deity as female. The culminating dance in this story is echoed by the dance in the story of the Cherokee Mother Sun. (See stories of the Mother Sun, Shapash, Sun Woman, and Saule.)

The Mirror Dance of Life

o one is alive anymore who can remember the time Amaterasu Omikami, the great woman who possesses noon, took herself into the cave of heaven and refused to come out. But to those who know the story, every mirror on earth is a reminder of that time and of the glorious moment she stepped again into the open sky, sending her surge of strength and will again through all life.

In those beginning times, the spirit of every living thing was called its *kami*. The kami of the mountain was lavender and long. The kami of the trees was great and green. Animals had kami in the shapes of swords and cups. Fish and flowers had kami. The kami of the rocks and the rivers were silent and calm. All the strength of these kami poured forth from the great mother sun, Amaterasu Omikami, and in her honor was woven the great pattern of the seasons of the planting and the harvesting of rice.

Amaterasu Omikami's brother, Susanowo, ruled the ocean. But he was jealous of the greater power of his sister, Amaterasu. Because Amaterasu knew of his ill feeling, she was suspicious when one day Susanowo sent word that he was coming to visit. Though she had a feast prepared on the day her brother was to arrive, Amaterasu also armed herself with a quiver of ten thousand silver arrows and a giant bow of beaten gold. She planted her feet firmly and awaited Susanowo.

But Susanowo came bearing gifts and speaking of trust and loyalty. Amaterasu and Susanowo ate together, and, after the meal had been cleared away, Amaterasu bowed to her brother. "How glad I am you've come in friendship," she said, her eyes shining. "I was worried you'd come otherwise."

Susanowo bowed in return. "Amaterasu Omikami," he said. "Let us forget the past. I have nothing but respect and admiration for you."

Late into the night they talked of their love for each other, their plans for the future, and the joy of their relationship. Finally Amaterasu bid Susanowo good-night and went to her cave to sleep.

Susanowo, however, did not go to bed. Instead he sat alone at the huge table, sipping sake and growing increasingly angry as he surveyed the beauty of his sister's palace. The memory of Amaterasu's graciousness grew ugly in Susanowo's mind. The liquor he drank slowly heated his resolve to show his sister who was really most powerful.

In the next few hours, Susanowo tore drunkenly through the plain of heaven. He piled mounds of dirt in the irrigation canals so no water could flow to the rice paddies. Not satisfied, he stomped on each and every plant until the fields were covered with broken and dying stalks. Then he took up the excrement of animals and humans and smeared it in Amaterasu's celestial weaving house where the heavenly women wove the sacred tapestries.

In fear and anger, the gods and goddesses went to wake Amaterasu. When the shining one saw what her brother had done, a pain stabbed her heart. Her hands hung limp at her sides.

"Susanowo!" Amaterasu's voice filled the plain of heaven like light suddenly fills a dark room.

Susanowo staggered into his sister's presence, pulling a piebald colt on a rope behind him. He spat on the floor of the celestial palace.

Amaterasu put her hands behind her back. "Susanowo, where are the words of last night?"

Susanowo spat again.

"Susanowo," said Amaterasu again. "You wrong me. But I ask only that you sleep. Leave off, brother. Sleep."

Susanowo answered by pulling the sword from his belt and whirling to plunge its blade through the heart of the colt behind him. Before the eyes of the entire heavenly court, he heaved the dead colt through the window of the palace and into the celestial weaving house below. There the carcass struck and broke the looms and sacred threads and sent several of the heavenly weavers to the land of the dead.

A cry of rage escaped the throat of Amaterasu Omikami. She ran from the palace and back to her cave. Once inside, she pulled the great door tight behind her and locked it, shutting away from heaven her warmth and light and plunging even the realm of Susanowo into darkness.

The gods and goddesses of heaven caught Susanowo, punished him, and banished him from heaven. But without Amaterasu Omikami to light the plain of heaven, there was only darkness. The kami of the rice withered. The kami of birds and animals, mountains and trees turned to gray ghosts. Life without Amaterasu Omikami was impossible.

The gods and goddesses gathered together to discuss how they might restore their precious Amaterasu Omikami. How to tempt her from her cave? How to let her know that Susanowo had been sent away?

"We must moan and grieve outside her cave. We must shout to her of our dead," said some of the deities.

"No," said others. "We must remind her of the joy she brings. We must dance for her."

And so it was that the dance of the mirrors was planned. All of the ghostly kami of the world gathered up what little strength they had left and pieces of shiny mirror. With the help of the gods and goddesses, they collected themselves outside the door of Amaterasu's cave and began to make a joyful noise. Songs and jokes flew, weakly at first and then, as the kami began to take strength from each other, more strongly. A dance bloomed, and deep inside the cave of heaven Amaterasu Omikami heard the voices of her people.

When Amaterasu cracked open the door of her cave, a slit of her brilliant light lit the night. When the kami felt the surge of life they had longed for, the dance became jubilant. Amaterasu listened and then poked her head outside the cave. At that very moment the mirrors of all the kami reflected back to Amaterasu Omikami her own stunning beauty, and Amaterasu Omikami stepped all the way out of her cave and into the open sky.

Once again the kami of the mountain grew lavender and long. The kami of the trees soared once again great and green. Animals again had kami in the shapes of swords and cups. The kami of fish and flowers and rocks and rivers swelled alive.

On that day the strength of all kami poured forth from the great Amaterasu, and in her honor was woven the great pattern of the seasons of the planting and the harvesting of rice. And so it is to this very day.

Ereshkigal, Queen of the Underworld and Inanna, Queen of Heaven

(uh-RESH-kig-gull) and (ee-NAH-nah)

Sumer

Introduction

C hristian storytellers borrowed extensively from the myth of Ereshkigal and her sister Inanna when they put together the story of the crucifixion and resurrection of Jesus. Indeed, it was Inanna, queen of heaven, who first taught her people how to die, be reborn, and rise again.

The stories of Inanna and Ereshkigal are recorded on cuneiform tablets dating up to 3,200 years before the birth of Christ. They come from Sumer, the most ancient literate civilization we know, today's Iraq and Middle East. Our knowledge of ancient Sumer is pieced together from the findings and interpretations of archaeologists and scholars, and Sumer's artifacts are still being discovered. These writings reveal the tremendous power of the goddess and her worship over time, as well as dramatic accounts of her conquer and the resulting emotional devastation of herself and her people.

Ereshkigal is the older of the two goddesses: her name appears in the oldest of Sumer's writings. She is queen of Irkalla, the land of the dead; queen of souls; the most merciful one. Her name Kigal means "great earth." Her counterparts in other cultures include Nephthys of Egypt; Persephone of Greece (see story); Kali of India (see story); and Hel of northern Europe, whose name Christian storytellers borrowed for the underworld they call hell.

Inanna, whose holy lap was the source of the earth's life blood (see stories of Danu and Juno) in the form of wells, rivers, and springs, was the most widely known goddess in later Sumerian history. Queen of Heaven, she was Venus, the morning and evening star, and was represented by an eight-petaled star, or rosette. (Both Amaterasu Omikami of Japan and Iamanja of Brazil are similarly associated: see stories.) Her animal counterparts were the snake, coiled on a staff, and the heifer, whose horns most probably represented the shapes of the moon and a woman's fallopian tubes. She is related to the Semitic goddess Ishtar and probably descended from the creator goddess Nammu, who was herself associated with the Mesopotamian Tiamat. The story of Tiamat, great mother of the sea, finally recounts her murder at the hands of male invaders.

As the myth of Amaterasu Omikami is a metaphor for the rice-growing cycle, the story of Inanna's descent and return from her sister Ereshkigal probably dramatizes the seasonal shift between the time of rain and plenty and the frightening time of drought and possible famine. The story of the seasons is perhaps the deepest one we humans know. It is no accident that Christian tellers who mapped for us the story of their Jesus pinpointed his return to life in the spring of the northern hemisphere. And, like the figure of Jesus, the Sumerian sister goddesses touch deeply the seasonal nature of our own personal psychologies in that far earlier version of this tremendous story of death and renewal.

Inanna's stripping of the seven articles of clothing may correspond to the dissolution of the persona by way of the seven chakras; her vulnerability, death, and rebirth metaphorically recapitulate a profound psycho-spiritual healing.

I invoke Inanna and Ereshkigal with bones, pits, and compost. I call on the sisters for help with grief, terror, loss, and healing. Ereshkigal is my ability to let truth be, without trying to fix or change it. Inanna is hope and the courage to move downward to change.

To Die, Be Reborn, and Rise Again

oon after the goddess Inanna, Queen of Heaven, took for herself the human Dumuzi as her husband, she heard that the husband of her sister Ereshkigal, Queen of the Underworld, had died.

Inanna decided to go to Ereshkigal and be with her sister in the underworld as she mourned. But when she called to her friend and helper Ninshubar to help her dress for her journey, she got an argument instead.

"Don't go," said Ninshubar. "Please, my Queen. Send your sister your sympathy by messenger."

"Ninshubar," said Inanna, "a message is not the same as my presence. I need to go to her."

"Beloved Inanna," said Ninshubar, "Ereshkigal sent you a message. You can send her one. I'm afraid she is queen of a realm that will take from you everything you have if you go. Inanna. Please. It is dangerous to go to Ereshkigal's underworld. The guards will take your fine garments. They will exact a price from you, Inanna. They may take your life."

"Ninshubar, I am going to go," said Inanna. "But I can see how worried you are, and so I concede this one thing. If I do not return in three days, send someone after me."

And so it was agreed. Ninshubar helped Inanna dress in garments that best proclaimed her Queen of Heaven. The starry velvet train of her gown floated after her as she and her servants left the realm of heaven and made their way to the underworld.

At the opening to the underworld, Inanna left her servants. "This journey I take alone," she told them, and began her way down to the palace of her sister.

When she had walked the first thousand steps into the earth, she came to the first gate. She could not see the faces of the guards there, but she could hear their voices. "Give us your crown," they ordered.

"Do you know to whom you speak?" said Inanna.

"We know," said the voices. "There is no passage here without a price. Give up your crown."

Inanna lifted the golden crown from her head and gave it to the guards. The gate opened.

Inanna descended another thousand steps. There was no light now, other than the light of her own self. She came to the second gate. Here the guards asked for her earrings.

"I do not plan to stay," said Inanna. "I am a visitor here only."

"Ereshkigal exacts payment from everyone who enters here. Even visitors," said the guards.

Inanna unhooked the jewels from her lobes. She gave them to the guards. The second gate opened.

At the third gate, Inanna had to give over her necklace. It weighed heavily in her hands as she passed it to the guards. The gate opened.

Inanna traveled another thousand steps deep. There they took her cloak with its starry velvet train. She shivered with cold. The fourth gate opened.

At the fifth gate, the guards asked Inanna for her diamond belt.

Inanna held her head proudly, but her voice trembled. "You have taken my crown and all of my jewels. You have stripped the covering from my shoulders and chest. Surely that is enough. You will not also take the belt that holds up my skirts?"

"The price of entering here is your belt," said the guards in voices that had no trembling. Inanna gave over her belt and held up her skirts with her hands.

At the sixth gate, Inanna said, "I am naked without my skirt."

"You must give up your skirt," said the guards.

Inanna wrapped her arms about herself for warmth and comfort. Her skirt fell to the floor, and she stepped away from it. The gate opened.

"This is the last gate," said the guards at the seventh gate. "To enter here, Inanna, Queen of Heaven, you must give up your last."

Inanna used her right foot to push the jeweled shoe from her left foot. But the toes of her bare left foot could not push off her right shoe. So Inanna bent and with both hands removed that last bit of covering from her body. The floor was icy cold. The last gate opened, and Inanna passed into the palace of the Queen of the Underworld.

There sat Ereshkigal on her throne. Her face was turned away from the door. Her hands lay limp on her knees. Inanna saw that the ceiling of the huge dark room curved over absolutely nothing except her sister on her throne, the coffin before her, and a basin of blood.

"Sister!" whispered Inanna.

The word echoed in the emptiness. "Sister!" said Inanna, louder this time. Her voice sounded small, and afraid.

Slowly Ereshkigal turned her face away from the shadows. Only her neck moved. The goddess's body on her throne stayed still.

Inanna walked forward in the cold with her hands outstretched. "Sister," she said. There were tears on her face.

Inanna stopped when her eyes met the eyes of Ereshkigal. Ereshkigal's face did not move. Inanna saw that in the center of each of her sister's eyes was a tiny human skull. Each of the skulls had eyes. All the eyes stared at Inanna.

Inanna fell to her knees. "Sister!" she cried. "You do not greet me and

21

I have come to comfort you! Sister, greet me! Let me mourn with you."

The terrible eyes of Ereshkigal didn't answer. They just looked.

"Ereshkigal!" cried Inanna. "Don't you know me? I am your sister!"

The mouth of Ereshkigal opened. "I know you," she said. Her voice was flat. "You are my sister, Inanna, Queen of Heaven, and you've come here to die."

"I've come to help you mourn, Ereshkigal. Not to die! To mourn! To cry with you. To hold you. Ereshkigal! Stop looking at me!"

Ereshkigal had moved her hands to the arms of her throne. Her fingers had curled in strength there and were pushing her body forward. Her eyes with the skulls in them seemed to pierce through Inanna. "No one escapes this house of death, Inanna. No one. You die, Inanna."

Inanna began to rock forward and backward. Her shoulders shook. Her neck arched. She tried to wrench her face away from the face of her sister. But her head was held in the force of the Queen of the Underworld's eyes. With a terrible noise, Inanna died.

Ereshkigal picked up the body of her sister in her arms and carried it to the wall. There on a giant hook she hung it and went back to sit on her throne.

Three days had passed back in the palace of the Queen of Heaven. Inanna had not returned. Ninshubar tied a knife to her belt under her skirts and went for help. She went first to one god, and then another. Both refused to help. Ninshubar began to run. Panting, she came to the house of Enkil.

"Enkil," she gasped. "Inanna has not returned from Ereshkigal. Please help."

Enkil was immediately alert. He poured Ninshubar a glass of cool water and bade her drink and rest. Ninshubar swallowed thirstily and began to breathe more easily.

"There!" Enkil smiled. "Now for help." He sat quietly for some moments and then looked at his hands. "Aha!" he said. "I know just the thing!"

From under his little fingernail he flicked two specks of dirt. He set them on the end of his index finger and blew them into the air. At once the two bits of dirt changed to two tiny demons with pointed ears, feet, and tongues. "Off with you both to the underworld," said Enkil. "Come back with our Queen Inanna."

The demons flew off on their tiny wings. Down they went, so small and quick that the guards at the seven gates did not even notice them as they darted through each gate's latticework.

In the throne room of Ereshkigal the demons saw a terrible sight. Queen Inanna hung rotting on a hook. Flies buzzed around her body. The basin of blood had spilled, and Queen Ereshkigal was hanging over the edge of the coffin at the center of the room moaning and screaming in pain and grief. The demons touched hands for a moment and then flew to each side of the sobbing queen.

"My husband is dead!" screamed Ereshkigal.

"Your husband is dead, O Queen," sang the demons.

"My husband is dead. My sister is dead. I am lower than low," moaned Ereshkigal.

"Your husband is dead. Your sister is dead. You are lower than low, O Queen," sang the demons.

"I am lower than low. My stomach crawls on the floor," moaned Ereshkigal.

"You are lower than low. Your stomach crawls on the floor," sang the demons.

Ereshkigal sobbed for a long time. The demons hovered quietly. For another long time, Ereshkigal lay quiet. Finally, she raised her head and looked at the demons. Her eyes were wet and deep, but there were no skulls in them now.

"Who are you?" asked Ereshkigal.

"We've come for Queen Inanna," sang the demons.

Ereshkigal hiccuped. "Your song is good, small ones," said Ereshkigal. "Help me take her down."

Ereshkigal and the demons lifted Inanna's body from the horrible hook.

"We have died together, my sister and I," said Ereshkigal. "It is the law of the underworld."

"Tell us the law, Queen Ereshkigal," sang the demons.

"My sister leaves. But the law is that she must send another in her place," said Ereshkigal.

"She must send another in her place," sang the demons. "That is the law."

So they took Queen Inanna's body back up through the seven gates. At each gate, the guards gave back Inanna's garments.

Then, at the opening to the upperworld, the demons waited and watched as Inanna revived herself. Awake and whole finally, she stood, and the demons bathed her and fed her. And when they had dressed her in all her finery, they told her Ereshkigal's instructions. "You must send someone down, O Queen, to take your place," they sang and flew away.

Inanna opened her arms to the trees and the sky and stepped one giant step into her palace. At the first archway, she met her brother, crying bitterly for the loss of his sister.

"Brother," said Inanna, "do not grieve. I am here! I have returned. Dance with me for joy."

At the second archway, Inanna met her son, smearing his face with ashes for the loss of his mother. "My son, do not grieve," said Inanna. "I am back! I have returned! Dance with me for joy."

Then Inanna saw Ninshubar. She took her friend in her arms and held her close.

"You have returned, my Queen," said Ninshubar.

"Where is my husband?" said Inanna. "I long for him. Where is he?"

Ninshubar looked away and shook her head.

"Ninshubar! Where is my husband?" said Inanna. "I will go to him in the fields with his sheep. How I long to be in his arms! "

"Inanna," said Ninshubar. "Dumuzi is not in his field."

"Where is he then?" asked Inanna.

"He is in your throne room," answered Ninshubar.

Inanna picked up her skirts and ran to the center of her palace. There on her throne she saw her husband. But Dumuzi was not crying. Nor was his face smeared with ashes. Instead Dumuzi was laughing and ordering the musicians to play another round of music. "Eat, drink, and be merry!" he shouted to the party of people. "I am king!"

Dumuzi stopped short when he saw his queen. Inanna's face had frozen hard. She stood very still.

"Inanna!" said Dumuzi. "You have returned! Inanna, I . . . "

Inanna pointed her finger at Dumuzi. "You," she said. "You. It is you who shall take my place with Ereshkigal."

The blood ran out of Dumuzi's face. "My Queen," he said.

"Queen Inanna!" A woman ran out of the crowd and knelt at Inanna's feet. "You know me. I am Geshtinanna, Dumuzi's sister. We were wrong not to grieve you, O Queen. But Inanna, we are human, and life seemed so short. We have danced and made merry today because we could die tomorrow. We were afraid, Inanna. O Queen Inanna, show mercy to me and my brother. Let us share the time in the underworld."

Inanna looked at Geshtinanna and then at Dumuzi. "So be it," said the Queen of Heaven, and she turned away.

So it is that half the year Dumuzi the shepherd spends tending his sheep while his sister lives in the underworld. The other half of the year Dumuzi lives in the realm of Ereshkigal while his sister, Geshtinanna, lives in the upperworld. Each year the brother and sister pass on the staircase of the seven gates and hold each other tightly before they separate again.

Hecate, Queen of the Crossroads

(HEK-uh-tay)
Anatolia

Introduction

Worshipped in both Greece and Anatolia, or ancient Turkey, the dark goddess Hecate was related to the goddess Hekat of the ancient Nubian people, the black-skinned rulers and people of Egypt. Hekat, oldest of the old, swam in water and walked on dry land. She was the magical essence of Au Set, the mighty mother of transformation, called Isis by the Greeks (see story.)

Hecate was goddess of the Amazons, the Greek name for the mother-worshipping nomadic tribes of women in North Africa, Anatolia, and the area near the Black Sea. Led by Hecate, commander of the mother's words of power, this fabled group of people once ruled over large parts of Asia. They may have been the first people to tame horses, and they were known for their physical and magical capacities to wage war. The name Amazon probably meant "moon woman," and some colonies of Amazons were said to live on women-only islands (such as Taurus, Lemnos, and Lesbos), consorting with males only when they wanted to conceive children.

Hecate's images and her magic cauldron were placed at threefold road crossings. For centuries her peoples invoked her protection when they traveled and left gifts at her road shrines on nights of the full moon. Her sacred hounds were said to bay hymns to her when she appeared.

Greeks associated their Hecate with both Persephone of the underworld (see story) and the dark side of the goddess Artemis: when the waxing huntress moon disappeared, the crone energy of Hecate, the dark moon, was said to take her place.

The European Middle Ages diabolized Hecate as queen of ghosts and witches. Catholic authorities said midwives, who were Hecate's wise women, were most dangerous to the Christian faith.

Hecate in this story invokes the beneficence of the crone (see stories of Baubo and Spider Grandmother) in order to begin to heal the image of old woman. We know of no crone more ancient than Earth herself, and some of my ability to be in relationship with the great wrinkled one depends on changing my relationship with my own and others' aging.

Offerings of bread or cake can be made to the Queen of the Crossroads for her protection for literal travel on the earth, and for figurative travel on this journey of life. Hecate helps me to find kindliness in my own agony of decision making and let go of that which I must in order to move on. She is my own tenderness and nurture in the middle of my nights. I invoke her during the waning or dark of the moon with a bit of fur combed from a black dog.

The Woman Behind
the Door of the Moon

n a dark Halloween night a long time ago
the sea was deep and black under the cape
of the sky. The waves swelled shimmery
green and crashed on the shore. Then
something else began to swell beneath the
waters. Thirteen silver fish boiled up to the surface of the sea and
flipped onto the land. The fish panted on the sand, and the moon
slipped into the sky from behind a cloud.

That was when the thirteen silver fish changed to thirteen huge
black dogs. The dogs leapt at the moon and then began to run. They
hurtled across the beach and onto the road where they ran and ran until
they came to the place where the road crossed with two others.

And there at the road crossing, the dogs began to chase each other
clockwise under the light of the moon. Out of the blur of fur and black
came something else.

Not fish, not dogs. This time girls. Women. Mothers. Cousins. Daughters. Nieces. Aunts. Grandmothers and granddaughters. Friends. All of them dancing and stepping high under the moon.

"Hecate!" the people shouted.

"Hecate!" they whispered. "Lady! Come to us!"

They tipped their heads back and called to the moon. Called to the round white circle in the black velvet sky.

"Mother! Hecate! Come to us!"

A door opened. Up in the moon, a door opened. The people on the ground below breathed. A ladder came out of the door. Rung after rung, it slipped through the sky. Finally it reached the ground at the center of the circle. While the people in the circle looked up, a figure emerged from the door in the moon and began to climb down the ladder.

The figure came closer and closer. And the people in the circle below began to see it was a Woman. Hooded and hunched. With a huge bag slung over her robes. Down, down she traveled, until finally she stood in the center of the people.

With both gnarled hands she heaved the bag off her shoulder. Then she removed the hood from her head.

A little girl said, "You're here!"

The Old Woman's face smiled. The moon lit the creases of her skin and the white mane of her hair. She opened the bag.

Inside were glasses of milk foaming just at the brims and chocolate chip cookies with raisins and almonds. For eating and eating and eating. The girls ate. The mothers ate. The friends and the cousins and the grandmothers ate. The aunts and the nieces ate; the granddaughters ate. They ate until they were full.

Then the Old Woman closed her bag. And she climbed back into the sky. She pulled up her ladder. And she closed the door. The moon glowed.

The women and girls below began to dance. Faster and faster they moved. A circle of light. Whirling round and round. And then black.

Furry and black. Thirteen dogs, howling at the moon. Then running. Bounding and leaping together. Away from the crossroads. Away down the road. Back across the beach. Then panting at the edge of the sea.

Panting and panting. Panting silver fish. Thirteen silver fish on the sand. Then a flinging of those fish bodies into the sea. The sea deep and dark under the cape of the sky.

And that's how it was on a Halloween night a long, long time ago.

Devi, Queen of All

(DEE-vie)
Hindu

Introduction

D*evi*, Sanskrit for "glowing with brilliant illumination" and cognate for the English word *divine,* is goddess of all the patterns of the universe. She is not external or separate from earth, she is the spiritual essence in all things that exist and occur.

The Harappans who first worshipped her in India's Indus Valley called her Danu, the same name used by the Celtic peoples of Ireland for their mother (see story.) The Harappans were practicing agriculture by 5000 B.C.E., and by 3000 B.C.E. had built large cities of two-story brick buildings. The people of the Indian Danu flourished for another thousand years before the Aryan invaders arrived in 2000 B.C.E. *The Vedas,* the earliest writings of the conquerors, describe the massacre and enslavement of the goddess worshippers by the Aryans, who enforced a caste system that subjugated dark-skinned peoples in the name of their holy male trinity: Indra, Mitra, and Varuna. Indra, the Vedic story goes, killed Danu, and patriarchy replaced matrifocal, earth-centered social systems.

Not for fifteen hundred years did the story of the great mother reemerge. In 500 C.E., storytellers from non-Aryan groups, who had lived only at the fringes of Brahmanic caste influence, put together the *Tantras* and the *Puranas,* new collections that painted the goddess once again as powerful, she who could obliterate the entire universe by closing her eyes even for a second.

Devi, they called her, the ultimate Shakti, the one whose image all other names and forms illuminate. Splitting the goddess into multiple aspects may have been a demotion in many cultures; the very same act, however, has also served to focus and clarify her immense complexity. As separate chapters in an epic story teach a whole worldview, so separate personifications of the great mother can paradoxically instruct about her simplicity. Knowing her as Devi, Shakti, Maya, and Kali (see stories), and by her hundreds of other names and forms, emboldens and humbles us at once.

The areas least affected by Brahmanic Aryan influence in today's India are the Malabar coast of the southwest and Bengal and Assam of the northeast. Malabar remains largely matrilineal and matrifocal, and the practice of polyandry (one woman having several husbands) was common until the twentieth century. Worship of the ammas—the mothers—is of primary concern there, and numerous woman poets over the centuries have thrived, more than one writing joyously of lesbian love. Tantric orders in Bengal and Assam include women in the highest clergy possible, and caste discrimination is discouraged.

I adapted Devi's traditional story from the one told in Merlin Stone's *Ancient Mirrors of Womanhood.* This story, in turn, was drawn from several books of the *Puranas.* I use a crown and a purple cloth to invoke her great centeredness in my life.

Devi and the Battle
with Durga the Evil One

nce, long ago in the heavens over the land of India, Durga, the Evil One, took the shape of a demon buffalo, raised up on his hind legs, and drove the gods and goddesses from heaven, forcing them to seek refuge in the forests of earth. Bellowing, he smashed the holy places and crashed through the skies to the earth below.

There Durga, the Evil One, stole fires from hearths, pushed great rivers from their paths, and dried up the rains. He uprooted mountains with his horns and dusted himself with the powder of gold and copper he found there.

The people cried out to the god Shiva. "Dancing prince! Save us from the monster Durga. Muscle the Evil One away. Tear out his horns!"

Prince Shiva was powerful, but he found the strength of his armies no match for the Durga. The demon buffalo continued his rampage.

Then the people gathered at the palace of the god Kalatri. "Guardian of the night," they called out. "Sneak up on the Durga. Tear out his tail from behind, and when he whirls to meet you, kill him with your power. We beg you. We are longing to be safe."

But Kalatri, too, found that his powers were nothing against the Evil One's storm. So the people gathered their jewels and went to the Devi. Into the circle of her throne room they flooded and fell on their faces before her.

Devi sat at the center on a throne, half of which was made of fire and the other half of water. A tree grew high on either side of her, and the scent of lotus hung in the air. Green threads sprayed out from her thousand hands, and Devi's three eyes glowed—one black, one white, and one the color of blood.

"Great One!" the people rumbled. "Luminous Mother! You of the thousand arms. Queen of Earth, Queen of Fire, Queen of Water, Queen of Air. You who hold the threads of all matter in your hands! Neither Shakti nor Kalatri can leash the mighty Durga. We need you, O Great One. Put your sword in his heart."

Devi, the Great One, rode to meet Durga on her lion. The demon buffalo had created soldiers beyond number for this battle. He also had one hundred twenty million chariots and one hundred twenty million horses. With a whoop of rage, the Evil One hailed a storm of arrows on Devi, but they fell from her body like raindrops.

Then the demon blew hurricanes with his breath. He tore boulders off mountains and uprooted trees. He hurled the trees and rocks at Devi, but they touched her like sand might touch a cliff in a breeze. Then the Evil One lashed a huge wave from the ocean with his tail and sent it to drown Devi's lion.

Though Devi's arms were busy with many battles, she was angered by the attack on her lion. She took a mighty rope and lassoed Durga's tail. At that instant, Durga the buffalo became Durga the lion. Devi plunged her sword through the lion, but Durga the lion then turned into Durga the man, sword and shield in his hands. When Devi slung her spear at Durga the man, Durga became Durga the elephant.

And so it was that the Evil One kept changing forms and creating more and more evil. No one lost and no one won. A mountain of evil grew up, and Devi sliced it into seven smaller hills.

Finally Durga showed himself in his true form. The demon buffalo stepped into battle without a disguise. This time he was Durga the Evil One, and he too had one thousand arms.

Then came the battle. One thousand arms of Durga flew against one thousand arms of Devi. Suddenly, just when it seemed that the clanging and cutting and searing could get no hotter, Devi stopped.

She pulled in her one thousand arms and sat herself down and was silent. Then slowly she spread a purple cloth before her and began to eat and drink of the fruits and wine that appeared there. Devi chewed and swallowed with pleasure, and her three eyes shone.

The whole world watched. People held their breaths. Why had Devi stopped fighting? Was she admitting defeat?

Then Devi stood. When she called to the Evil One, her voice sounded like cymbals and bells. "Durga! Laugh your last laugh!" she said.

Durga roared.

Devi leapt up and set her foot on his neck. Then with her thousand arms, she tore the thousand arms of the Evil One from his body. Then she braided his arms into her hair until they rose up like a crown about her face.

The people cheered. "We are saved! Victory! Queen of the World! Savior! Devi!" they shouted, waving branches and singing.

From that day forth, Devi was called Devi the Luminous by her people. But they also called her Durga, for at the battle of the buffalo demon they saw Durga become a part of the Devi.

II

Constant Change

The Everlasting Cycle

The slender greens gloving the narcissus buds shrivel in order to free the blossoms.

The circle of death to life and life to death again is sacred. Death is not a punishment from the goddess: it is the culmination of a process that endlessly repeats itself on the smallest and largest scales. The universe that is essentially *being* is also in constant change. Patterns of light rise and disappear over the course of a day. Baby is now child; the girl bleeds for the first time; the friend betrays; the career shift is made; we lose the fantasy and adapt to the reality.

Goddess lore mythologizes her shape-shifting: when portrayed as sun, we understand her as the yearly changes that nip and warm us; shut us inside, and pour us outside again. When she is moon, she merges continuously into different phases of herself: she is new, then waxing large; she is full; she is waning and dark. As moon, she has three faces: maiden, mother, crone.

As the new and waxing moon, she is maiden-virgin. Her territory her self, she explores free of other than self-commitment. Though she may be relational and even sexual with others, her knowing comes from the pool she gazes into alone. The virgin turns corners and travels new paths. She fiercely protects the child. Virgin is creator: out of nothingness, she brings forth. Now is the time for wishes to collect strength; for affirmations to take action.

As full moon, she is mother, preserver, realizer. Keeper of the mundane, her territory is transition. Unlike the focused attention of the virgin, the mother's awareness is diffuse, taking in the whole picture. She is abundant: adjudicating, laughing, ministering, cooking all at once. She is the luminous center of the cycle that has begun in nothing and will end in darkness. This is the time for stock-taking and -making, giving thanks, glowing in the complexity of our lives.

As old one, waning moon, she is crone, the ancient ender. She has birthed and buried the loves of her heart; killed what needed killing. She has sat with the doomed and the usual and can let the child sob on her lap. She tells the truth; she is the undertaker of dreams; disillusion is her realm. Now is the time to let it come apart, to let go of what we once were sure we could not live without.

Everything on earth instructs us about her everlasting, cyclical change. We take in through our mouths and let go through our anuses, over and over again. Our hormones peak and drop daily and monthly, spiraling us through energies and moods. Relationships ebb and flow. We are productive and inspired; we lie tiny and fallow. The garden explodes, weedy and full of feasts; it lies rotting and dense until we begin again. Days pass in sevens; months curve around us and turn into years. Workplaces shift personnel, customers, products; establishments become memories and certainties only photographs. The once young are now elders; the once little are now feeding their own. Waves of politics come and go. Departures, tornadoes, thefts, and divorces smash our hopes, undo our routines, leave us stunned, panting, and simple to begin again.

Anyone who has chanted knows that chanting past the point of boredom deepens its power. Anyone who has stared from the edge of a cliff at the waves below knows the peace that comes with endless crashings and silences. How comforted we humans are with the table set the same way for the holiday, the story told for the twentieth time, the line quadrupled in the poem. Our deepest rhythms are cyclical and repetitive. These are the rhythms of the goddess. Despite our habitual difficulty with honoring death, depression, and despair, we humans pass our lives unable to avoid the endings that make way for beginnings. In the maturity of goddess sight, we come to hold the completions as sacred as the starts.

In the context of the cycle, it is easier to accept the endings. We make our rituals circular: we sit in a circle; we make a beginning, a middle, and an end; we promise each other we will meet again. We set the ritual in the context of the cyclical year. As far as we city folk dwell from the beat of agricultural life, we can still comprehend at least eight points in the turning of the great wheel of life. Outside and inside, our year begins, like life itself, in the dark. In the northern hemisphere, Halloween or Samhain (SOW-when) (October 31/November 1) is our New Year. Like a seed in the ground or a fetus in the womb, our hopes and joys are conceived in the dark. At New Year the veil is very thin between ourselves and the ancestors; between what has been and what will be in our lives. Winter Solstice (December 21), the shortest day, heralds light's birth; now is the time to cradle the new. At Candlemas or Imbolg (February 1), our dreams are toddlers, rollicking potentials with already strong personalities. Spring Equinox (March 21), when day is of even length with night, honors the sassy and confusing puberties of our projects and ourselves. Beltaine (May 1) couples us and all that we yearn for with the forces of life. At Summer Solstice (June 21), the longest and the strongest of the light, we are overflowing with concerted effort. On Lammas Day (August 1), even we supermarket customers take the time to honor the myriad fruits of the farmers' labors and our own. At Fall Equinox (September 21), when the night is again even with the day, we watch the brightness of the light turn milky in the cooling air. Time for self-assessment: we are beginning to move into the dark that will start the cycle once more.

Nothing we plan, say, or do has any effect on these perennial changes. Earth turns always, travels her orbit, carries us with her. Perhaps we working, singing, meditating creatures are her consciousness. Perhaps it is through our emotional perceptions and expressions that earth knows her own wonders and sorrows. She is the great process out of which we come and to which we always return.

Danu, the Earth

(DAN-oo)
Ireland

Introduction

Despite increasing industrialization, today's Ireland is famed for her still-told stories of fairy mounds and little people in the grass. Today's tales are earth-magic remnants of the sagas of human-sized, magically powered queens, kings, heroes, and heroines that preceded them. These stories, in turn, recapitulate the even older tales when goddesses and gods, representing the powers of earth, water, fire, and air, peopled the world. The tellers of those ancient stories called themselves the *tuatha de Danaan,* or the tribe of the goddess Danu.

The Irish Danu, Danuna, or Dana shared her name with forms of the great mother in cultures around the world, such as the Danes and the biblical Danites (called "serpents" by writers of the Old Testament). The Russians called her Dennitsa (see story of the Zoryas); the classical Greeks named her Danae; the Hebrews Dinah; and the Babylonians called her Danu or Dunnu.

Although the ancient tuatha de Danaan named the earth goddess as the very source of their lives, Danu is rarely mentioned by today's authors trying to piece together the myths from that time. Instead, most stories told today emphasize the role of Dagdu, the sun god. A traveler to County Meath in Ireland can, for example, visit Newgrange, a beautifully preserved tomb built in the form of an underground temple in 3000 B.C.E—or five hundred years before the erection of the pyramids. The entrance stones are inscribed with giant spirals, and the damp, cool passageway to the center is now rigged electrically to expose spirals and inverted triangles etched on the inner walls. The guide also uses an electric light to reenact the nearly miraculous once-a-year flooding of the dark center (through the window in the roof) with the light of the rising sun on the morning of the winter solstice. The sense of being in a womblike place is overwhelming. The literature provided to Newgrange visitors, however, fails to note this palpable reality. Instead, it first praises the high degree of architectural, engineering, and artistic skill displayed by this ancient crop-raising people, and carefully notes the measurements and placement of roofbox, chambers, great circle, and surrounding standing stones of the Great Mound. The pamphlet's author then declares that Newgrange is a monument to "no less a personage than the chief of all the gods," Dagdu the Sun.

I wrote the story of Danu the Earth after a moving visit to this underground temple. Unlike the pamphlet's author, I had to ask myself why a people would build a monument to the sun inside the earth in such a way as to take the light of the sun into its depths for only minutes each year.

I was further inspired by my visit to the bowels of Dublin's museum, in which are gathered a dozen or so of what curators call "sheila-na-gigs." Sheila-na-gigs are stone figures of squatting women displaying their sometimes red-stained vulvas. As late as the Middle Ages, these figures were carved above church entryways. Both these churches and their startling guardians were built by medieval goddess-worshipping villagers in the process of overlaying their own spirit life with Christian dogma. Danu, I have no doubt, was a figure much like the far more modern sheila-na-gigs, who almost certainly represented the womb and tomb as the single point at which meet life and death in the great mother's cycle.

Here is the story of Danu's filling the world with her rhythm, that she might surge always in the blood tides of our bodies and hearts. How sweet to carry menstruation from a medicalized sanitation to a tender sanctification.

The Gift of
Rhythm and Blood

t the beginning of the beginning, the goddess Danu glittered tiny as a fairy in the mists. You'd scarce have seen her, even had you been there, for the swirl of milky gray about her gossamer self. But Danu was there, sure as we're here, a glistening globe of possibility at the start of it all.

It was Danu's dreamtime then. Asleep, her thoughts quivered and swelled. Awake, she held her face in her hands, wondering and humming, lost in her own stillness. It may well have been the dreams that caused the growing. The dreams trickled at first and then flooded in the pearly dark place between sleeping and waking, where time is like water and nothing is impossible. But whether it came from the dreaming or something else, Danu the goddess grew. Oh, it surprised her how she grew!

It was her legs at first. She extended them and splayed her toes. Somehow those spread toes came to hold whole bays between their peninsular lengths, and her limbs stretched lopingly long. Hard and round and luscious they'd become—with knees and thighs fair like mountains, they were so huge. Her arms shot from their sockets and came to end in gigantic slender-fingered hands in which she could suddenly see the streams and creeks of veins. The once plump little wrists took on the definition of hills—and, oh! the down of her forearms resembled meadows more than anything. Her neck, too, had lost its cushion and got a swivel to match the capacity of her stride.

How shy this Danu, how astounded! How full of her change she was, once wee as an idea and now enormous as the world. She had flitted once, effortlessly. Now her movements felt tremendous and heavy. Musing, she drifted finally into a sleep of exhaustion, only to wake to even more growing.

Danu opened her eyes to the sight of dark green sprouts on the soft triangle below her navel. Gingerly, she fingered these spiky curling firs and delighted herself when they didn't fall away. More sprang up, in the valleys under her arms and on the lush three-sided range between her legs, until those sweet places were most forested with trees.

Then, before she slept again, Danu's breasts grew. Gone were the days when she could arch her chest and describe a smooth bridge between belly and neck! Now that arch was soft and spilling as twin mountains tipped by red wild flowers!

When Danu plunged again into sleep, she dreamed this time of a great ball of fire in the sky that splintered the mists around her as the music of a pipe and drum filled a silence. When she awoke, her haunches felt sure and deep and she found a river of blood flowing between her legs. Danu tasted the scarlet wetness in wonder and turned her eyes to the sky. Immediately, she was sugared with a yellow warmth, and the skin of her shoulders expanded with pleasure.

"You're my dream!" she cried out, and her eyes glinted in the light.

"I'm your dream," a voice agreed. "I am Dagdu the Sun."

Danu cast down her eyes, and her smile dazzled when she turned them up again. "Do stay, Dagdu the Sun," said Danu the Earth. "I can't tell you how good you feel!"

"Oh, I will stay, lovely green, brown, and red Lady!" said the voice. "I will stay."

Danu sighed and turned over. Dagdu the Sun broke all the way through the mists and poured down on the body of the goddess. She fell asleep there in the heat. Who knows how long she slept, but when she awoke this time, Dagdu was gone. Danu sat up and caught up the back of her hair in her hand. She looked at the silvery clouds and remembered Dagdu's delicious warmth. Then she looked down and put her hand on the place where the river of blood had come. How soft and good it felt there! The wetness lay in a pool beside her, but it had ceased to flow. She moved her hand up to the wings of her pelvis and then dipped them again to the cave between her legs. For surely that's what she felt: a deep, wet cavern that nestled in the protection of the mountains of her bones.

How pleased Danu was to see her Dagdu again! For in his absence, she'd begun to think of him that way—as her Dagdu, her wonderful sun whose light would shine especially for her delight. Not far from the truth, either, that way of thinking, for it happened that Dagdu himself came to think never so clearly as when he imagined his Danu and felt never so free as when he held her in his arms. For that's what became of the friendship of Earth and Sun. They talked to each other; they traced each other's noses and bit each other's palms. They made each other shout with laughter. One day Danu told Dagdu about the dark, secret place under her forests. Dagdu's voice was tender when he asked if he could look inside.

It was Dagdu who told her about the smooth, round globe at the back of her cave that changed again and again from pale mauve to the color of wine. For Danu did finally invite Dagdu to flood her dark with his light, and it was once in a reverie that followed a time when they had held each other in this way that Danu had her dream of making animals and people. She awoke flushed and intense with excitement. Dagdu kissed the ridge of her cheek when she told him and plucked away the damp tendril of hair that clung to her forehead. "It's a wonderful dream," he said.

On the evening of the day Danu followed her dream and formed animals and people of the soft earth of her breasts and the pool of blood beside her, Dagdu told her that she'd never looked so beautiful.

"When you pursed your lips like that and set the people moving with your breath! Hmmmm! The scent of you, Danu!" he said, and nestled his head in her neck. The sky grew soft and pink around that comely couple while they watched the animals mew and burrow for cover and the humans sing tunes and smear their mouths purple with currants.

Perhaps an eon passed before Danu and Dagdu had the argument. Couples will argue, you know, much as they may also please each other, for they are not one but two beings and so they are bound to see and feel things differently. But isn't it true that the argument that makes one so cross at the time can, not so much later, be the inspiration for wonderful change? It was certainly that way with the argument of Danu and Dagdu, for out of their misunderstanding came the very rhythm of our world.

Danu had been dreaming again, asleep in Dagdu's embrace. She jerked awake suddenly one night, shaking with the cracked pieces of a nightmare inside her.

"Dagdu!" Danu's voice was sharp.

"Hmmmm?" Dagdu's voice was dim with sleep.

"Dagdu. I dreamed that my people forget me." The god heard the fear in Danu's voice. He lay his finger on her lips and made hushing noises while he rocked her against him.

Danu returned to sleep, but she spoke urgently again about the dream in the morning. Dagdu toyed languidly with her little finger as she talked. "What was it, darling?" he said.

Danu couldn't remember the images. She just knew it was a terrible feeling of dread she had and this knowing that her people had forgotten her.

"Darling, they're not going to forget you!" Dagdu said soothingly. "You *made* them."

"I can't explain it," said Danu. "But it was as if the people—I think there were thousands of them—as if they thought I were dead, but I was really alive. It was horrible." Danu turned her head away.

Dagdu curled four of her fingers around one of his own. "Danu, they can't forget either of us," he said. His voice was teasing. "They certainly can't forget me, anyway. I'm much too hot and warm, and I feel too good."

Danu snatched her hand away. Now Dagdu had meant, I'm sure, to nuzzle her with his teasing and relax her with his caresses. However, Dagdu had not dreamed Danu's dream, and Danu's averted head prevented her from seeing the playful sympathy on Dagdu's face. She heard only the lightness of his mood in contrast to her own despair, and she was furious.

A black wind came up and the goddess stayed alone for a long time. She wept and slept. She screamed and dreamed. She felt the curve and the flatness of herself. She watched her blood river come and go. She spoke aloud and unraveled the horror of that nightmare about a kind of aloneness not healing and full of truth like this one, but dangerous and a lie.

Slowly there grew in Danu a plan, details blurred at first. But came the day when it was clear and simple as if she'd known it all along.

First she reached inside the cave of herself and drew out the globe that Dagdu had told her waxed and waned with a cycle he said seemed to match her desire to lie in his arms.

She gazed at it, now creamy and gray in her palm, and remembered the uninterrupted mists of her beginnings. Then she hung it in the sky and called it moon.

Next Danu called to her all the people that had breasts and valleys like her own. Like herself, she told them, they would bleed, in rhythm with her moon, rivers between their legs so that they and those who love them might ever remember her. Like herself, they would find refuge in both the light and the dark.

Danu's plan thrilled her people. In their village, they made a temple like Danu's cave with long narrow windows to welcome Dagdu's light.

They drew on the walls there the story of the ebb and flow of the blood river by counting its days with careful marks. They pecked its clock with circular spirals on giant stones. They painted red the door of her sacred triangle to mark the place from which all had come and to which they would return.

Danu, too, was filled with peace. Maybe you can imagine the speechless shyness with which she reopened her friendship with Dagdu. How the words tumbled when the shyness melted. And how much they had to tell about what each had learned in the time of solitude and introspection. Time passed and they repeated the cycle again and again. It was true, they agreed. Never did they feel so verdant, so radiant, as when they came together again after the renewal of separation.

And so it was with Danu's humans. Never did the world throb so rightly as when the people remembered to sing in the cave of their goddess and to dance in the light of their god. Ever through time has circled this remembering, even in the days when the people, as Danu once dreamed, are so close to forgetting her. But her wonderful plan, born in the contemplation of her terror, prevents forgetting. For in the bodies of Danu's women flows her river, and in her sky moves her moon. And so for women, and all those who love them, the goddess lives. Tiny as a fairy in the mists, perhaps, or gigantic as the world. She lives.

Kali, Dancer on Gravestones

(KAH-lee)
Hindu

Introduction

Although most commonly understood in her destroyer aspect, the goddess Kali is Hinduism's full triple goddess. She is the ocean of menstrual blood at the beginning of time, out of whose nourishment comes all life. She is the mother fountain of endless love, and, in the same way that the monthly blood shedding of a human woman destroys the possibility of life for a cycle, she is the ender of all. She is the hungry earth, who devours her own children.

Like Maya, Devi, and Shakti (see stories), Kali is the primordial feminine, out of whom all comes and to whom all returns. It is in her destroyer aspect, however, that she most upsets the colloquial image of the goddess in the West. Her squatting, many-armed form, with her bared teeth and necklace of skulls, with the corpse of her consort Shiva beneath her, defies once and for all our stereotype of the goddess as a combination of nymph, Cleopatra, and Florence Nightingale.

In relationship to the corpse god Shiva, Kali is the aspect of the goddess Shakti that precedes and follows another revival of Shiva as lord of the dance: she is the goddess alone in the majesty of her totality. For the god Shiva, along with his masculine counterparts, Brahma and Vishnu, is like the water contained in the hollow made by a cow's hoof compared with the vast sea of their goddess.

To write the story of Kali, I took my notebook and pen on a walk in Oakland's Redwood Park. I had spent the evening before whispering her name, asking help. How could I accessibly portray this disturbing goddess along with the profoundly nonpunitive Hindu sense of death? I left the trail to sit cross-legged under deep shade in piles of evergreen needles. I chewed the pen's cap and felt the dark around me. The draft story came, and, with a sense of peace and accomplishment, I rose to return home. My clothes were covered with tiny white maggots: Kali was here.

Kali's colors are red, black, and white. I invoke her with knife, skull, or cauldron.

The Story of Death

here is not enough room!" the people were crying. "There is not enough room!"

It was true. Plants were so thick on the forest floors that the strongest knives could not cut paths through them. Corn and rice grew so high in the fields that they towered like trees over the people. People had not enough to eat in those times, because no one died. Babies came and grew bigger and bigger, but people did not get old and they never left the earth.

That was when the goddess Kali turned over in her sleep. The peoples' cry, "There's not enough room!" became part of her dream. But she must have been ready to awake because the next cry, "There's not enough room!" woke her and she sat up.

"You disturb my sleep!" she bellowed, rubbing her eyes with her fists.

"There's not enough room!" the people cried.

Kali drew on her robes. She walked to her window and threw it open to look out on the world. She put her dark hands on the sill and leaned out. Her black hair ruffled in the wind. What she saw made her draw back.

Kali saw crowds of people piled on each other, none of them old, all of them elbowing each other to get at vats of food in buildings crammed together so tightly it was hard to see the sky. Animals swarmed through the throngs. The air was hot with sweat and perfume and soil.

Kali licked her lips. Her hands went to her hips. "Time!" she yelled.

Her servant, Time, came running. "Bring me my red sari," she ordered. Time brought the garment, dark as the color of blood.

Kali threw off the gray robes of sleep and fastened the scarlet about her. "Clothe yourself," she said to her servant. "We are going out. And bring me my jewels."

Time did as bidden. He took up her gray robes for himself and put on shoes in the shape of fish. Then he brought Kali her necklace, swinging with skulls.

"Take these," Kali said, and she thrust gifts wrapped in golden paper into Time's hands. "Now call my chariot!"

The chariot came, pulled by eight white stallions and eight black mares. Fire leapt from its wheels when Kali and Time climbed to its platform. With a loud cry, Kali raised her hand and let loose the rein.

The horses smoked across the distance to earth. Before each village, Kali drew in the rein. Her servant Time stepped from the chariot and handed the goldwrapped gifts to the people who crowded at each stop.

In each package the people found Kali's gifts. Mildew. Mold. Disease. Decay. Worms. Beetles. Rust. Rot. Aging.

It was on that day that crops knew more than just blooming and growing. They knew also the withering that returned them to the soil. It was on that day that the plants of the forest floor began to add to the blackness of the soil so the trees could grow.

Animals had babies, but now the babies grew old. Humans, too, began to age. They also began to die, so there would be room for their children.

Kali and her servant Time returned to her palace. Exhausted she fell, still crimson-clothed, across her bed. Time undressed her gently and tucked her under the covers.

Kali is the goddess who dances at funerals and sometimes stops babies from being born. Kali still rides with her servant, Time. Since that first trip, though, Time has carried his own presents. Time gives people the gift of white hairs, and he wraps them carefully in the gold paper of wisdom and acceptance.

Changing Woman

Navajo People

Introduction

The Navajo of southwest North America call the processes of nature Estsan Atlehi: Woman Changing. In the person of Changing Woman, the Navajo anthropomorphize nature and remind us, in turn, that the tick of our human natures resembles none other than earth's endless fluctuations. The Navajo see her, as do the Arunta of Australia (see story of Sun Woman), as able to metamorphose endlessly, becoming both young and old again and again.

Embedded in the wisdom of Changing Woman is also the truth that she cannot be defied. To the people who taught us this way of seeing earth, Euroamericans owe a great debt they are just beginning to realize. For despite vast differences in language and social structure, the peoples we today call Native Americans, who migrated to North America at least twelve thousand years ago, revere the living world. They use night dreams as sources of wisdom and respect plants and animals as teaching spirits. Their traditions can show us the ways of walking lightly on the trail of beauty called life on earth.

Changing Woman's story is a retelling of her traditional myth as related by Merlin Stone in *Ancient Mirrors of Womanhood*. Changing Woman's power and comfort is the unrelenting constancy of her shifts. I invoke her by placing a ring or hoop on my altar. Sweeping and mundane, her presence works in my life. I have tried to convey her dependable as a bathrobe wrapped around me while the hotcakes steam.

Between Things
That Are Different

as the question "Why?" ever split you like a bent fork and left you shiny and pointed with pain? Perhaps the phone rang then or the laundry needed drying, and the pulse of the world pushed the why behind you.

Has the why returned later, but this time flat and quiet, still with you, but not twisted in the same way now?

There is a very small pocket of time between the sharp question and the event that makes you forget. Into that small pocket of time the goddess Changing Woman flies. Changing Woman flies in, and she fills up the pocket.

Changing Woman comes to stay in spaces of time between things that are different. She is there between the clocktime start of the weekend and the bodytime start. She is there between the time you choose your trip's destination and the moment the seat belt fastens about you for your journey home. Changing Woman fills up the time after the fitful, sobbing nights and before your cactus soul bursts into pink blossom again.

Changing Woman is hard to see. The pockets of time she lives in can be fleeting, and she is always moving. Sometimes she's beside you, sometimes she's underneath you, and sometimes she's inside your heart. Sometimes she's in yesterday, and sometimes she's a few minutes from now. Sometimes she is Girl, other times Teenager. Sometimes she's big and strong. Other times her hair is snow white and she walks with a turquoise cane.

At the beginning of the world, Changing Woman kicked and gurgled. In the pocket of time at the beginning, before the mountains heaved themselves out of the mist, Baby Changing Woman laughed and clapped her hands in a basket of red flowers. When the mountains humped up high, Baby Changing Woman shouted and climbed from her basket, changing from Baby to Child. The winds and rains came to play with her. Child Changing Woman sang, and grasses blew in the valleys. Trees popped from the hills.

In the pocket of time before the sun came out, Changing Woman turned into Girl. She kicked over the basket of red flowers and scattered the petals. Everywhere a petal landed, an animal sprang up. The petals on the land grew beaver, buffalo, squirrel, and grasshopper. The petals on the breeze flew into birds. The petals in the water dove into fish.

While the animals turned into parents of eggs and fluff, Changing Woman became Woman and walked a trail of beauty in the world. She turned her neck this way and that. "I see ten thousand things," said Woman Changing Woman. "They are beautiful and I am glad."

Now Changing Woman grew hungry. She killed a buffalo and cooked the meat for her meal. She made a bed of the shaggy fur and slept for many nights and days.

When she awoke, Changing Woman soaked herself in a side pool of the sunlit river. Now she was scrubbing and rubbing her dark skin with buffalo's fat. Now she was Mother. Men and women slipped from between Mother Changing Woman's thighs. Children sprang from her belly. Turning her neck back and forth, Mother Changing Woman watched her people build homes and make families.

Changing Woman's skin withered. Wrinkled Changing Woman taught the people how to plant kernels of corn, how to pick the sweet yellow ears, and how to grind the dried corn into meal for cooking. Wrinkled Changing Woman gave the people songs for being born, songs for growing up, and other songs for dying. Old Woman Changing Woman gave the earth the time of hot and the time of cold.

When the people see Changing Woman in the time of hot, they call her Mother and feel her strong muscles pounding the laundry white at the edge of the river. When they see her in the time of cold, they call her Grandmother and feel her thin and frail as she walks oh so slowly across the snow.

People come to Changing Woman for many things. "Teach us to weave, Changing Woman. Teach us to gallop," the people beg. And in the time between the tangled skeins and the blanket, in the time between the clumsiness of two and the ripple of one running, Changing Woman is at work.

"Changing Woman, why death?" asks a girl. And between the dying and the seed planted at the burial, Changing Woman is there. Changing Woman lives in the time of wet faces. Changing Woman is there when the seed bushes into tree.

"Changing Woman, what is this life about?" ask a man and a woman. "We don't understand."

That's when Changing Woman looks like Girl. Only her teeth show that she is old. When she smiles, they are full of gold.

Changing Woman gives each a red flower. "Come with me," she beckons. "Come walk with me on the trail of beauty."

In the pocket of time between the asking and the asking again, the woman and man walk with Changing Woman. On the trail of beauty with Changing Woman, the people walk. On the trail of beauty, the people see, hear, feel, taste, and smell all of the ten thousand things.

Isis, Queen of the World

(EYE-sis)

Egypt

Introduction

Like Freya of Scandinavia and Juno of Rome (see stories), Isis is the Greek name for the Egyptian goddess of the thousand names in the completeness of her majesty. Queen of healing and magic, mistress of the gods, Isis of Egypt was actively worshipped for three and a half thousand years, nearly twice as long as Christ. Pyramid texts of 3000 B.C.E. refer to the "Great Isis," and the final suppression of her official worship came not until 426 C.E., a century after Constantine had declared Christianity the acceptable religion of the Roman Empire. Her geographical range was enormous: when Alexander the Great conquered Egypt in 332 B.C.E., he spread the word of the Mother of Life from emperors' palaces to private homes and marketplaces, until finally her honor reached from Egypt to the River Thames in London.

Called Au Set by the Egyptians, Isis, separator of heaven and earth and inventor of agriculture, sheltered the pharaohs in her winged lap. In the myth that recapitulates the death and resurrection of the annual vegetation cycle, Isis is sister-wife-mother to Horus-Osiris, the male god who dies as a seed is buried in order to return again to life with the flood of her water. (See stories of Ereshkigal and Inanna, Demeter and Persephone, Shapash, and Mayahuel.) Indeed, the overflow of the Nile River is said to be her tears of agony as Isis searches with her sister Nephthys of the underworld for the pieces of her Osiris, killed and mutilated in a rage by Set, the god of destruction. The sister goddesses re-member Osiris, and Isis, pregnant by the revivified god, gives birth to son Horus, who is his father's reborn self.

Isis, the compassionate one, she who has suffered (see story of Kuan Yin), also reigns over all that is miraculous, even as the endless cycle of the harvest never ceases to bless and astonish. Present at childbirth and guide on death's journey, Isis satisfied humanity through her humanness, and her realm came to include even the sea as people of many languages and locations clasped her to their hearts. Isis is the Black Madonna of today's eastern Europe and, with her son Horus, the prototype of all Christian madonna-child images.

I use feathers to remind me of the winged arms of Isis, which represent to me her power to comfort, protect, and to soar in transformation. I wrote her story to invoke the intense personal humanity of her presence.

The Story of Life

orus-Osiris the Land sat in the lap of his Mother, Isis the River. Cuddled there in her great winged arms, Horus-Osiris heard the story of life. Isis told Osiris about the stars and about the wind. She told him about wisdom and healing. She told him of turquoise and sailboats and the sticky brown date fruit in the desert.

"And me, Mama?" asked Osiris. "Tell a story about me."

"You, Osiris," said Isis, "are the keeper of all the plants and seeds of the world."

"Like the barley and wheat?" asked Osiris.

"Like the barley and wheat," said Isis. "Like the little barley and little wheat that must cuddle in the dark till they grow big enough for people to pick and eat."

"I am little now," said Osiris. "Am I like a barley seed?"

"Yes, just like a barley seed," said Isis.

"Mama, will I get big like the barley and wheat?" asked Osiris.

"You will get big, my son," said Isis.

"Will the people pick me?"

"The people will pick you."

"But Mama, I will be in pieces then! And if people eat me up, where will the new little barleys and wheats come from?"

Isis hugged Osiris very close. She kissed him many times on the top of his head. Horus-Osiris wiggled to look at Isis. "Mama! Why are you crying?"

"I am crying, Osiris, because you will grow big and you will go away from me. The people will pick you, and you will be in pieces. And I will miss you. . . . But . . ."

"Mama! I don't want to go away from you!" Osiris wrapped his arms tightly around his mother's neck.

"But, Osiris, I will pick a piece of you, too. And I will swallow you down to my lap again—just like we are now."

Osiris pulled away from Isis and looked for a long time at her face. Then with his fingers, he petted the soft feathers of her wings.

"Mama, will I get big like that soon?"

Isis sighed. "Soon enough, son," she said.

"Mama," said Osiris, "if I get big, then little on your lap, will I get big again?"

"Yes," said Isis.

"And then little, and big, then little—over and over?" asked Osiris.

"Over and over," said Isis.

"Will you always remember to swallow me when I'm in pieces?" asked Osiris.

"Always," said Isis. "I will never forget."

"Mama," said Osiris, "Is that because we're magic?"

"Yes, my son," said Isis. "It's because we're magic."

"Good night Mama," said Horus-Osiris, and he put two fingers in his mouth.

"Good night, Osiris," said Isis, and she folded her wings over her son to shut out the light.

The Three Zoryas, Keepers of Dawn, Day, and Night

(ZOR-yahs)

Slavs

Introduction

The Zoryas are goddesses whose mythology is rooted in the northern Slavic land of the primeval forests. In Russia, for example, the forest is the nursery of culture, and its beauty and danger color customs and stories. Food and friendship are hard to find in that cold, dense land, and its peoples compensated by developing warm traditions of hospitality. Life in the frozen forest was built around the dwelling in the clearing and its source of heat. Indeed, heat, not light, is the way to the spirit.

Slavic peoples in these regions dealt with harsh seasonal cycles; the ebb and flow of nomadic conquerors; the constant possibility of fires gone out of control; and insects and rodents gnawing up from below. In this beautiful but unfriendly context was born the triple goddess known as the Three Zoryas or the Dawn goddess (Zorya Utrennyaya); the Morning Star goddess (Zvezda Dennitsa); and the Sunset or Evening Star goddess (Zorya Vechernyaya.) The myth of the Three Zoryas gives them responsibility for keeping the Dog of Destruction tied securely to the constellation Ursa Minor, lest it run loose and end the world.

The ancient religions of the Slavs respected natural processes: the ripening as fruit ripens and the growing as grass grows. They kept alive a passion for seeing beauty and spiritual truth in concrete rather than abstract forms. While writing the story of the Three Zoryas, I felt as if I were painting instead, so tangible did I feel their loving, steadfast, absolute warmth to be. Sometimes I make tea and do housework, very slowly, in honor of the Zoryas. I use a piece of rope on my altar to symbolize the strength and flexibility of their boundary-keeping.

The House of Heat
for the Beloved Visitor

t the top of the forest that reaches the heavens live the Three Zoryas, who endlessly tend the dawn, the day, and the night. Safe from the fighting, the frosts, and the fires live the Three Zoryas in a dark wooden hut next to the corral of the sun. Ever heating in that hut is the stove on which swells hot bread and steams the samovar for tea for the beloved visitor.

"Stay! Stay!" welcome the Zoryas, soaking traveler's blue hands and wet feet in in hot water, then bundling them with fur. They give her the place of honor right next to the glowing heat.

Over and over again the Zoryas renew her tea; they light a beeswax candle and make ready for her a bed of piney boughs. No matter the length of time that passes here in this fragrant home, the visitor is warm and fed; always she is safe from the fighting, the frost, and the fires.

And no matter the length of time that passes here, always

Grandmother Zorya is first up at the dawn. White haired and slow moving, she kindles again the stove. No matter the pain in her hips that morning, Grandmother Zorya leaves the hut at the break of light for the corral of the sun horses.

She croons softly to them as she unlatches the ancient gate. They are nickering and nibbling at their troughs, and their faces are beautiful and aware as Grandmother Zorya's wrinkled hand lets swing the gate. The colder the air, the slower she moves, but finally, never failing, she opens the gate. Like the burst of energy from a hot popping log, the white horses break and snort and plunge, rippling and smooth, into the sky with the light of the sun expanding pink and aqua about them. Grandmother Zorya returns then to the hut, where she sets the samovar to boil.

Early or late the sun horses may have begun their gallop, but always the Maiden Zorya makes her way, too, into the day. When the visitor follows and climbs the hill behind the hut, she may see the Maiden Zorya setting out against the immaculate liquid blue of the sky. Or, on a day when the air is cold, Maiden Zorya moves quickly, and sometimes the visitor can barely discern her thick bundled form against the clouds. The winds then drown any sound of the sun horses' hooves and the visitor returns early to the warmth of the hearth.

But on a day when the hooves still echo to the listener on the hill, Maiden Zorya is a dream of muscle and laughter in the field below the stable flung wide, where even the new fallen dung smells of the fresh air. There that sturdy Maiden Zorya tosses the heavy yield of the hay while the poppies seethe in the open space and the birds grow fat on wild berries. If she disappears, perhaps she is gathering mushrooms, moss, or bark deep in the forest. But always she returns in the soft or the swelter: the moss will cover the floor of the hut, the bark will make shoes and paper.

The thoughts of the visitor might whisper on this day. Or, for the colors alone, she might break into song. Sometimes the visitor might nap with her Maiden Zorya, right there on the billow of the green hill while the plums on the tree overhead purple in the light.

No matter whether the time is passed hunting in the cool green leaf of forest, or reaping in the yellow ocean of rye, always the strength of the Maiden Zorya spends itself finally and she and her visitor walk arm in arm back to their supper.

The birch trees at the edge of the corral are dappled and their leaves take on the sheen of fading light. Mother Zorya, keeper of the night, covers her head against the deepening chill and walks slowly to the gate of the corral. She readies the water and the hay for the tired animals. Closer and closer trot the horses of the sun. The sunlight behind them is like a cut melon, delicious and cold in the paling sky. Whinnying greeting, flanked in sweat, the sun horses fill the corral with their aliveness and Mother Zorya shuts firm the gate. Perhaps she stays inside the corral to brush the coats of the animals. Perhaps she just sits, still and silent, watching the quiet animals sink their noses to their feed. The light is dove colored now; shadows melt and mingle, colors mute. The visitor inside the hut feels a longing and a sadness in her chest.

Mother Zorya must do another task before her never-failing work is done. The horses are fed and watered; the gate is shut tight. Now she must feed the dog chained to the iron stake at the sky place where the stars take the form of the Little Bear.

The visitor is wistful. She wishes Mother Zorya would hurry with her errand. She will be able to drop away to sleep only when all Three Zoryas sit together by the crackling hearth. She offers to help Mother Zorya carry the bucket of scraps to the dog in the sky.

Together they travel. The darkness is gleaming now with stars. The visitor feels afraid when she sees the dog. The dog is thin. It strains at the chain, teeth bared, hairs high on its neck, ears back. Mother Zorya calls softly. The visitor hangs back and watches. Mother Zorya heaves the contents of the pail before the dog. The animal tenses. But its ears are forward now and its eyes are sad. Mother Zorya talks gently. The dog throws itself to its meal.

"No matter how much it eats, it is always hungry," says Mother Zorya. "It is the dog of agony and destruction. Always it is afraid, but always I come. I never forget."

The dog seems sated now. It is lying down. Only its hindquarters are tensed. The visitor feels a lump in her throat. She returns with Mother Zorya to the hut, empty bucket wobbling between them.

Embers glow, sinking to ashes. The Zoryas—Grandmother, Maiden, Mother—sing the visitor to sleep. The sun horses stand, leaning their big heads on one another in the dark.

That visitor might be you. The Zoryas make you welcome any time. They are delighted to see you. There in their hut, safe from the fighting, the frosts, and the fires, you may sip the tea of their cheerful little samovar. It is there you may repair when you need to firmly shut the gate of your corral, to say no, this is done, this is enough. It's time to eat and be inside. Or it is there you may go when it's time to open your gate, to let the flood of your expression and strength prance, wind playing in the fine hair of your mane. Or perhaps you will linger inside the hut, because timidity and hopelessness fill you. Perhaps then you will remember to feed the dog who strains at your chain, whose eyes turn from wild to lonely and whose fears you may quiet for a time with your devoted attention. Perhaps you will visit that hut of the Zoryas because they are the limit setters, the boundary keepers, and you need their unflagging responsiveness to the slow rhythm of your day. Maybe you will come when it's hard to say yes. Then Grandmother Zorya and Maiden Zorya will help you fling your gate and fill your sky. Maybe you will come when you are terrified to say no and the unknown snarls before you like the fangs of a beast. Then Mother Zorya will help you shut your gate and feed the endless questions until the morning comes.

Shapash, Mother of Radiance

The Levant

Introduction

In this story, one of the oldest in the world (see also story of Ereshkigal and Inanna), kindly and powerful Shapash the Sun is the final arbitrator in the battle between Baal, prince of life, and Mot, prince of death. The discovery in 1928 of the Ras Samra Tablet in northern Syria opened for us a new understanding of the mythologies that both predate and coincide with biblical myth. The goddess, known as Ashtart, Astoreth, Astarte (see story), Atargatis, Asherah, Aral, and Shapash, was worshipped in the Levant, an area we now call Lebanon, Israel, and Syria. The Ras Samra Tablets, badly damaged and written in what looks like cuneiform but is actually an alphabet, is composed in a language we now call Ugaritic. Their stories, including this one, dating from the fourteenth century B.C.E. have much earlier origins.

Baal, prince of fertility in this story, later supplants the father god El and comes to be identified with so many different deities—including the Hebrew Yahweh—that his name comes to mean simply "Lord"—a composite of many gods. "Baal" or "Baalim" appears repeatedly in the

Old Testament as the name of the "false" gods of the "others." In Arabic, rain-watered soil is still called "land of Baal," while arid, barren places are called *mawat,* a cognate with the name Mot, prince of sterility. The "waterboy," Ashtar, in a role doubtless filled in other versions of the story by the goddess herself, represents the power of artificial irrigation. *Athtari* in Arabic still means soil so watered. Anat, goddess of love and slaughter, is Baal's sister, and Astarte, his beloved. Like the Greek Persephone (see story) Baal eats of the underworld's food and is thus compelled to an everlasting cycle of return and departure (see story of Innana.) Shapash, quietly splendid, is unique among the gods and goddesses in this story because of her ability to travel freely between the upper and lower worlds. Shapash, the steady one, is keeper of the balance between our famines and our feasts.

How Shapash
the Sun Rescued the
Prince of Fertility

aal, cloud rider, prince of rain, gazed out of
the great window of his new palace. Yamm,
the sea dragon, was dead and Baal was king
of earth now. Without competition from
the ocean god, Baal could send through his
window the snow, rain, and moisture in every right season.

Baal, perfumed with myrrh, arrayed in robes of silver and white,
turned to look at the seven hundred seven golden tables of his victory
feast. Here were the rarest of wines, the crispest of breads, the plumpest
of quince and raisin cakes, the most tender of meats. Heavy with satisfaction, Baal belted and braceleted himself with the vines of the grape
and wore narcissus for his crown.

Now his guests began to arrive: Kothar the smith, decked in sprigs
of pale-blue—berried juniper; his sister, Anat, teeth white as a flock of
goats, in jeweled pomegranate gowns; Ashtar, the water boy, eyes

shining with reverence. Thousands of the heavenly ones thronged Baal's hall.

Then Shapash the Sun arrived, the rays of her golden crown splashing the hall with her glittering warmth. On her arm came old Father El, lord of the mountain, dignified, cheeks ruddy, in his mottled blue robes.

Now came Baal's beloved, for whom he'd fought the monster Yamm: Astarte, hair black as night and studded with diamonds. Baal took her hand, flushing proudly, and ordered the musicians to begin.

"Seventy times seventy!" he roared.

"Long may you live!" his guests thundered.

Baal's wine slid silken down his throat. Contentedly he looked about the clinking, laughing, reveling company.

But suddenly a draft pierced his shoulders. No one else seemed to notice. But a fearful thought slithered into his peace. In the midst of plenty, these friends, this triumph, there intruded into Baal's mind the picture of the one god whom he had not invited. Mot, drought maker, king of the underworld, was not here.

"Yamm the sea dragon is gone," Baal told himself. "I must not think of Mot. He doesn't deserve to come." He downed his chalice of wine and reached for Astarte's hand.

"What is it, my love?" asked Astarte, lips beautifully full.

"Mot," said Baal.

"What about him?"

Baal's brow knitted. "Could Mot at this very moment be plotting to take my place as ruler of earth?"

"Send him a message, darling," said Astarte. "Ashtar!" she called to the water boy, who sat near Kothar the smith. The deities relayed her call until Ashtar came running to Astarte's side. "Go to Mot, boy, and take him this message from Baal."

Ashtar's eyes widened.

"Tell him that Baal is supreme. Tell him that Baal will pay tribute to no one." She smiled at Baal, but saw that the corners of his mouth were flat. "Go!" she said to the water boy. Then she touched Baal's lips with her fingertips. "Now dance with me," she said into his ear. "All is well."

But Baal shouted after the water boy. "Ashtar! Mot lives under the mountain with the twin peaks. Lift up the mountain and descend and take my message to Mot. But whatever you do, don't get too near his throne, or he will snatch you like a lamb between the jaws of a lion. Tell him Baal is king."

The water boy sped away, and Baal danced in Astarte's arms.

When Ashtar finally returned, the party was over, and the dining room empty of all but Baal. Ashtar knelt among the clutter of gnawed bones, goblets, and fruit pits sucked clean of their flesh. "What did Mot say?" asked Baal.

"My lord, Mot is angry. He knows about your feast, my lord. He says that if you will not have him as your guest, he will have you. He says you may imagine he has mud and filth to feast on, but he will heap on you such fare as you have never tasted before."

Baal felt the chill again at his back. "I dare not go," he muttered. "Mot will kill me if I go to his palace."

Ashtar raised his face. "Oh no, my lord. You are king of the world, my lord."

But Baal summoned messengers from the vineyard and the meadow. "Flatter Mot and win his favor," he told them. "Bring him the most lavish of your gifts. And tell him I am his servant, his devoted slave!"

But Mot refused Baal's gifts. "He says you are a coward, my lord," said the messenger of the vineyard. "He says you try to insult him and that you have no mettle." The messenger of the meadow nodded. "He is very angry, my lord. He dares you to come to his table."

Baal saw that he would have to confront his rival. He painted his face with red ocher as a charm against the forces of death. He rallied the clouds and the winds to carry seventy bushels of silver coins as gifts; he placed weapons on the seat of his chariot.

Baal heaved up the twin peaks of the mountains. Their soil stayed in his fingernails and streaked his face and robes. The clouds and the winds left the silver coins with the first of Mot's guards. Baal strapped his weapons to his waist and entered a maze of darkling steps that wound deep into the earth. It seemed that Mot's guards had known he was coming, for at each of the seven iron gateways, they saluted respectfully. Noting this friendly reception, Baal grew calm, even confident, as he descended.

Even so, he was not prepared for Mot's graciousness. "Baal!" said Mot, warmly, soothingly. "You have come so far! You will want to bathe before you eat. I have drawn a bath for you!"

Indeed, steam curled from a long tub that crouched on birds' talons. The king of the underworld's smile was ghastly and his body skeletal under his loose-hanging robes. Except for his purplish eye sockets and the spots of red color on his cheeks, Mot's face was white as lime. His lips were bloodless and his teeth brown and sharp. But his looks stirred in Baal more pity than fear, and he wanted to believe in Mot's sincerity.

"He's lonely," thought Baal smugly. "I should have come a long time ago. He is much easier to handle than I'd thought."

As Baal's eyes grew accustomed to the dimness, he saw beside the tub an iron table on which had been laid a sumptuous feast. He laid down his weapons and gratefully settled himself into the hot water. Soaking in the tub, he found himself enjoying a conversation with his enemy. The days of brooding about his fate slipped away, and his body relaxed. By the time he had emerged from his bath and rested, he found himself ravenously hungry.

But Baal forgot that whoever eats of the food of the underworld may nevermore return to the world above.

Mot's eyes glittered with approval as Baal heaped his plate. When Baal had tasted his first morsel, Mot threw back his head and laughed. "Now you are fully welcomed, my friend!"

Baal felt the sleep of death steal over him. Not even his misjudgement of Mot mattered to him now.

At once, earth above began to languish. No rain fell, no green thing grew up. The clouds and the winds, waiting beside Baal's chariot, looked at each other uneasily. When the corn in the field before them shriveled on its stalks, they raced to the throne of Father El. Breathless and distraught, they fell before him. "Sire! Baal has sunk to the underworld! We wait for him and he does not return! The fields are dying! There is no rain!"

Old Father El started from his throne. "He has eaten of Mot's table, I know it!" he rasped.

The clouds and the winds lay limp before him. "We fear it so, Sire. We fear it so."

Father El ripped away the shoulder of his azure robe. Down he came from his throne and rubbed ashes upon his head. "Baal is dead!" he raised his voice in lamentation. Down from his mountain he stumbled, over and over calling his mournful song in the fields and the valleys. "Baal is dead! Baal is dead!"

"Noooooooooo!" screamed Anat, the sister of Baal, when she heard Father El's words. Like a ewe bereft of its lamb, she moaned. She tore her flesh and searched for her brother with a wild and frantic keening.

Shapash the Sun heard her cries. "What is it, Anat?" she asked kindly.

"Lady Sun," said Anat brokenly. "My brother is dead. He never came back from Mot, and I cannot even find his body for a funeral."

Shapash leaned closer. "Is Baal in the underworld?"

Anat tensed, startled by a sudden hope. "Yes, my Lady! Shapash! You are the only one of us who can go and return from Mot's realm. Shapash, my Lady, will you go and look for Baal and bring him back to me?"

Shapash's face glowed with sympathy. "I will go, Anat. I will return with Baal's body."

Shapash left. Night plunged over the sorrowful Anat, weeping now in relief. Already no green thing grew, and while Shapash searched for Baal, neither did the earth have light.

Shapash finally returned with Baal's body in her arms. The musicians of Baal's party now played dirges, and the gods and goddesses who had

danced and feasted now rent their clothes and wept. Sadly, not knowing what else to do, they made Ashtar, the water boy, king of the land.
But alas, Ashtar's head could not reach the top of Baal's throne, nor
could his feet touch its footstool.

Anat found Mot, prince of sterility, strolling through the dead fields
of earth. The lord of death did not even have time to cry out. With a
roar of rage, Anat pushed him to the ground, ripped him to pieces with
her sword, burned his flesh in fire, and winnowed him with her breath,
ground him in a mill, and sowed him into the earth.

That night, the gods and goddesses dreamed of rivers running with
honey, clouds raining soft oil, green plants bursting with milk. Baal
woke from his death as from a sleep, and Shapash the Sun took him up
again, this time alive, in her arms.

The Lady Sun carried Baal to his palace. Astarte kissed his brow, his
ears, his lips. Ashtar the water boy climbed down from Baal's throne.
Anat washed her brother's feet, fed him, and perfumed his hair. Baal,
prince of fertility, waxed strong again, and the gods and goddesses
rejoiced.

But deep in the earth, where Anat had sown the pieces of his body,
Mot also revived. Out of the earth Mot sprouted, rising again in his
ancient form. "Baaaaal!" he roared. "Come and fight!"

Long and fierce was the battle of the prince of death and the prince
of life. They pranced like antelopes, gored like bulls, charged like stallions, and stung like asps. Now Mot triumphed, now Baal.

At the height of their fury, Shapash the Sun raised her voice.
"MOT!" she cried out.

The prince of death lay gasping on the ground.

"Mot! Leave Baal to the upperworld and return to your own abode,"
ordered Sun. "The time has come for life. Go, Mot, or every god and
goddess will pluck up the foundation of your house and break your
sceptor."

The light from Sun blinded Mot. Baal stood panting, while Mot,
covering his eyes, rose and conceded the fight. "Let Baal be king," said
Mot and turned away.

Baal fell on his face before Shapash the Sun. "I am your servant," said the king of the rain.

Shapash the Sun smiled. Warmed and strengthened, Baal raised himself up and walked, his step increasingly light, away to his palace. There he would send through his great window the snow, rain, and moisture in every right season.

III

Spirit Incarnate

Goddess As Earth and Body

I n Mexico, I was struck by the slang *carnal* (accent on the last syllable) used by men to call a buddy something equivalent to "brother" or "bro." It seemed a wonderful word to me: the word "carnal" in the fundamentalist Christianity of my youth had always been spoken in the same breath as sin. In phrases that never failed to make me uneasy, ministers would explain that we Christians were not to be "of this earth, earthy," and that we were to "put away the things of this world."

My body, in the religion of my childhood, was a trap. Though we called it a "temple," I was taught that it would betray me and lead me astray from the "paths of righteousness." Because, like most children, I was interested in feats of prowess, conquering my body and its desires appealed to me. Especially in settings in which grownups were unable to acknowledge, let alone meet, my needs, why not just get rid of needs? Why not accept a philosophy that made desire and sensation the lowest of the low on a hierarchy that conceived of even the word base as bad?

Living in my head made a lot of sense in a context in which physical and emotional feelings appropriate to circumstance were not allowed. Sensation would just get me into trouble, I reasoned. My religious teachers must be right. Better I should make my highest concern control of my body and feelings.

Such a mind-set was abetted, of course, by the larger, secular culture. Just as the religious culture equated the color black with sin, the secular culture associated black with bad, dirty, and ugly. The religious culture admonished control of the body; the secular culture pressed the same restrictions, particularly on people labeled as more "physical" than "mental": children, women, and people of color. Ferret out what needs fixing and adjust it. Tone it down, keep it together, sit up straight, be quiet, and keep a smile on your face. Erase yourself.

Earth, like body, in this culture of control, is a list of resources that need managing. Look nice but don't cause trouble. Across history and in the present time, peoples who do not have controlling relationships with earth identify with her instead. Earth is alive; there are spirits in rocks and rivers. Throughout the history of control culture, the stories of people identified with earth have been crushed, their images misshapen, and their lands taken for "resource value." Like the minds and bodies of girls, women, and people of color, earth herself has been stripped, raped, poisoned, desecrated, and left for dead.

But like the people who are her consciousness, earth has begun to rise again. Over and over again I hear the stories of people, otherwise steeped in rational, left-brain thinking, who feel they hear the call of the great feminine flow of life, asking them to stand and create for her. Left for dead she has been, but she has not died. Like a part of ourselves crushed or swollen, shaking with effort, she is reviving herself. She is calling racism, sexism, classism, ageism, homophobia, and colonialism by the name of body hatred, and she is linking the politics of control back to the abuse of herself. She is making us wonder how our personal insistence on consumer convenience is really different from the sense of entitlement with which the corporate colonizer turns a forest into a beef ranch. She is promising us that feelings count: the agony and the anger show us where we stand. She is assuring us that our desires help us clean our house: pretending we have no needs is a recipe for victimization.

Goddess is earth. She is incarnate. She is knowing, willing, daring, and silence. She is east, south, west, and north; thought, spirit, feeling, body. Out of her silent north body coils east's knowing. Out of the knowing blazes south's will. Out of south's fires flood west's daring waters of change. North's body accepts the imprint of her change. In silence comes again east's mindfulness that bends south's will and frees west's daring. And so it is.

Nu Kua, Great Snail Woman

(new-KWA)

China

Introduction

P re-Buddhist creator goddess, Nu Kua, precursor to Kuan Yin (see
story), is said to repair the universe when it shatters, and to estab-
lish the harmony and balance of the world. She sets the seasons in order,
thrusts the planets and stars on their proper courses, and may well be
the personification of the gently omnipotent nature written about in
the *Tao Te Ching* by, presumably, Lao Tzu (meaning ancient teacher), in
600 B.C.E.

Texts as ancient as 1000 B.C.E. (Chow Period) refer to the Snail
Woman who also takes the form of turtle and fish. More details come
from the later Han Period (200 B.C.E.–200 C.E.) from the Hopei and
Shansi peoples in an area once known as Chi'. These writings tell of
her creation of the world and then her reparation of its breakages
during "The Great Cosmic Struggle" of 2500 B.C.E. She is the
essence of the patterns. Her activity is like water that flows around
instead of crashing against. Goddess reverence for the ancient

Chinese and for today's student of the Tao is about the emulation of the ways of nature and the coming to peace with her subtlety and paradox.

I invoke Nu Kua with chanting and a spiral-shaped shell.

In the Beginning

n the beginning, the world was a green purse, a tiny green round house, a turning rounding curling shell of a world that was wet and dark and full of mucus. In the beginning was the purse shell house of the world curling in the sticky cool dark of the river making the wake of the Snail Woman. In the beginning thick and dark, silver and black, was the Woman Snail, the Nu Kua, the keeper of the deep. In the beginning in the rounded whorled conch lived Nu Kua, the waker of all the makings of the world. In the beginning, under the cool green of the spreading moving icy green was Nu Kua, beginner of the song of life. Out of the bowl of her purse house self, out of her sticky wet night, out of the green of her home in the green, drew Nu Kua the reed organ of life. Onto the organ she blew, into the reed, onto and into, flowing, forming, singing, moving, slipping into and out of the river, inching and quivering and soaking out sky. Soaking out fishes and turtles and eggs, limpid for birds and the rice and the eel. Blowing her reed curled the Nu Kua, humping and slipping and pushing out life. In the beginning was the Nu Kua, everywhere flowing, everywhere making the ten thousand things. In the beginning silent and tiny, in the beginning without aim, in the beginning nourished Nu Kua the ten thousand things. Nu Kua, greatest of all, tiny and without form. Nu Kua, great because she is not great, is the mystery green center of the story of life.

Freya, Mother of All

(FRAY-uh)
Scandinavia

Introduction

Like Au Set of Egypt, called Isis by the Greeks, and Juno of Rome (see stories), Freya was the northern European goddess whose totality of power was worshipped by her peoples, even when they called her by a hundred different names. Widely revered by country people for centuries after states had claimed Christianity as the official religion, she was a reality with which Catholic authorities in Germany, Scandinavia, and Iceland had to reckon. Recognizing that prohibiting her honor altogether was impossible, the church both co-opted and diabolized her symbols. Thus, for example, they taught that Friday, Freya's sacred day, was really a Catholic holy day on which fish, one of her sacred animals, was to be eaten. And they plunged her magical number thirteen into disrepute. Luckiest of lucky, Freya's thirteen, the number of the moon and menstrual cycles in a year, became the number to be shunned, especially when it fell on Friday, which would have doubled its power for her worshippers.

Like other forms of the great goddess, Freya was identified with the land itself. She was thus the embodiment of sexual love, tenderness, beauty, and nurture, as well as the mud of the underworld, the tomb of all living. The sow, known for her tremendous fertility, the usefulness of all her parts to humans, and her ability to compost even her own feces inside herself, was another of Freya's symbols. Her priestesses, women known as the *volva*, functioned as both oracular wise women and judges of her principles of right living, justice, honor, and peace.

Freya's story is my variation of one found in the thirteenth century C.E., *Prose Edda* of Snorri Sturluson. I turn to Freya to overcome my despair about earth's bondage. I invoke her with images of the globe, the pig, the black cat, and the number thirteen.

The Story of Who
Owns the Land

he old ones say that Freya, Eartha, mother of all, goddess of the plow, mistress of cats, she of the sacred thirteen moons, goddess of love, the great sow mother, comes riding on Fridays to dispense her wisdom to those who seek it and to engentle the lives of those weary in body and sick at heart. It is on Fridays that the people eat of her sacred fish, bathe themselves in perfumed hot waters, and cling to their beloveds with sweet abandon.

Freya comes riding, they say, in her chariot of light, drawn by thirteen cats as sleek and black as night. Swift and silent she comes, they say, to those who call out her name for comfort and truth. So quick and noiseless is she, they say, that always some forget her power and forget to call out her name.

That is so now, and it was so even a thousand years ago on a Friday night in the dead of winter, under the shining moon.

Two neighbors stood there in the snow shaking their fists and shouting at one another. Friends and relatives bundled in furs circled them, stamping and calling punctuations to their fight.

"This land is mine, fool!" yelled the taller, whose name was Angantyr.

"It's mine, I tell you," said Ottar, the other. He put his face close to Angantyr's and jabbed his finger. "And even if it weren't mine, Angantyr," hissed Ottar, "I'd take it from you!"

"I'll use whatever I please to grow my crops on my land, Ottar," rasped Angantyr.

"No poison!" yelled Ottar.

"No poison! No poison!" The friends of Ottar took up the cry.

The argument had begun three years before when Angantyr began to use poison to kill weeds and insects on the rich black land. Angantyr said poison made his work easier and gave him a bigger crop. Ottar said easier or bigger, he didn't care. He would have no poison in his soil, and he said the poison there leached into his water too. Ottar brought a rabbit he'd found bloated and dead to the house of Angantyr.

"See what your poison does, Angantyr? Take your poison and get out!" he had ordered.

"You get out, Ottar, if you know what's good for you," Angantyr had responded, slamming his door in Ottar's face. And the two neighbors had bickered and raged at each other until tonight, when they stood, sticks in hand, under the shining moon.

"Wait," said a hoarse voice. The excited folk moved aside to let an old woman make a path to the two angry men. The people recognized her by her voice and her limp as the one the goddess speaks through. They saw that with her she dragged a huge bag that twisted and grunted with a live thing inside.

"Ottar and Angantyr," she wheezed. "Freya shall decide on the question of your land."

The group of neighbors crowded close, and a noise rose up among them when the old woman opened the bag. Out of the opening and onto the snow lumbered a huge mother pig swollen with the babies she had inside her.

"Freya," the old woman whispered. The light from the moon shone down on the white and pink of the sow's back, and the animal stood perfectly still.

"Freya," whispered the people and stepped a little away.

Ottar and Angantyr stood breathing hard, but quiet now. The old woman looked sharply at Ottar and then Angantyr and pulled from her hands the skins that covered them. Slowly the two men knelt in the snow. The old woman set a hand each on the shoulders of the kneeling enemies and looked up at the moon.

"Freya!" her voice quavered in the stillness. Then a shudder passed through her. "The rightful owner of this land knows who has owned this land before him," she said. "The one of you who can name the most names of the owner shall own the land. You shall have until the next full moon."

The old woman dropped her hands.

"So be it!" said the people and dispersed into the night.

Angantyr and Ottar spent the next month gathering the names of the owners who had come before them. People buzzed with opinions and conjectures about which of the men would have the longest list. Some said Angantyr was sure to win, as he had the best memory. Others said Ottar should win because he loved the land best.

"It's not a matter of love!" said others. "Freya requires the names of the owners who came before. That is all. Whoever has the longest list shall own the land."

So the Saturdays and the Sundays, the Mondays and the Tuesdays, the Wednesdays and the Thursdays, and the Fridays rolled around and away. On the night of the next full moon, the people gathered in a barn at the edge of Ottar and Angantyr's land. When they arrived, they found that the one the goddess speaks through was already there. By the side of a small fire she knelt, next to a mound of hay on which lay the great mother sow. At each of the huge pig's thirteen teats suckled a tiny white and black piglet. The stillness, filled only with the crackle of the fire and the grunts of the babies, was broken by the tramp and bustle of the people. Only when Ottar and Angantyr came and the old woman rose did the people hush.

"Freya hears you now, Angantyr," said the old woman.

Angantyr puffed out his chest and cleared his throat. "I have searched," he said loudly. "By listening to the elders, by reading the records, and by my own memory, I know the ownership of my land backward for seven generations."

A ripple of approval moved through the friends of Angantyr. Seven generations reached far back into time, and if Angantyr could name those names, surely he would win. Ottar could not possibly name names farther back than seven generations.

In a proud voice, Angantyr recited the names of the owners who'd come before him, calling each one the son of the next. His friends cheered when he was finished.

"Freya will hear you now, Ottar," said the old woman.

Ottar, too, cleared his throat. "There are twenty generations right now on my land," he said. "And each of those generations who owns this land goes backward to the beginning of time."

The people's voices rose. What could he mean? Twenty generations? When Angantyr had had seven? Impossible. Ottar was lying.

"Wait," said the old woman. Then she called for another stick of wood for the fire. "Speak, Ottar," she said. The people silenced themselves.

When Ottar spoke, he did not name the human names of a line of fathers and sons. Instead he named the mold and the mushroom, the worm and the grass, the insect and the herb, the spider and the flower, the bee and the mouse, the mole and the minnow, the turtle and the frog, the snake and the tree, the squirrel and the rabbit, and the fox and the hawk.

"They are the owners of the land," said Ottar. "Then and now and forever."

And so it was that Ottar that night won the argument with Angantyr.

Never more, while those men lived, did poison for weeds or insects spoil the soil and water of that place.

Things were different in older times, the old ones say, and some are sure that such wisdom is never more to be heard from the great sow mother.

But there are those who swear that on a Friday night, especially a Friday of the sacred number thirteen, the wisdom of Freya, the great sow mother, can be had by those who call down her chariot of light drawn by her sleek black cats whose eyes wink slow as the stars.

Shekina, Keeper of Wisdom

(shuh–KEE–nuh)
Hebrew

Introduction

People who are uncovering psychological and spiritual truths experience the power of knowing something in the body—not just in the head nor even only in the heart. Jewish mystical writings, called the Kabbalah, used the word *daath* for the insight that is true because it is accompanied by great feeling. *Daath* is the knowledge that comes from the union of conscious and unconscious minds, a kind of knowing that is at essence erotic. *Daath* is also the word used by Kabbalistic writers to refer to the union of God with his bride, the Sabbath, or the Shekina. The *Zohar*, the principal book of the Kabbalah, says, "[On the Sabbath] all is found in one body, complete, for the Matronit clings to the King and is become one body, and this is why blessings are found on that day."

Shekina, meaning Sabbath, is the name for the Feast of the Full Moon, which once celebrated the menstruation of the great goddess. Originally honored once a month, her holiness came to be observed once every quarter moon, or once a week. The Friday evening that began her honor was the night in which the husband of the home made love with his wife, recapitulating the union of the god and goddess. The following day, Saturday, was devoted to the postcoital reverie of washed perceptions and the leisurely depth of feeling that should not be disturbed by mundane doings or materialism.

Patriarchal influence, however, lessened interest in the power of love between the male and female deities within and outside of humans. Consequently, the Sabbath became more an observance obsessed with the minutiae of the law, and the Shekina, once goddess of Babylon and then of the Jews, went underground.

Her light still glows, however, in the holiness of passionate love, and the braids of her hair are suggested in the shape of challah bread. Study of the Torah, said to be her outer garments, can be symbolized in erotic imagery: like a bride within her curtained chamber, the Shekina must be courted with the heart, soul, and entire being of those who would know her wisdom and joy.

Silver candlesticks, white candles, and challah bread all help me to call the Shekina. I wrote this story from the point of view of the young ascetic in me who is still waking to the peace of her own body. Sections of *The Wise Wound* by Penelope Shuttle and Peter Redgrove were invaluable for my understanding of the Shekina.

The Door to the Soul

nce a young man asked himself these questions: Who am I? And how am I connected to all others? He wondered and wandered and asked the questions again and again. He yearned for the answers.

One day he approached a teacher and asked, "Who am I? And how am I connected to all others?" The teacher said, "Study will answer those riddles."

"What must I study?" asked the young man.

"Study the thousand and one books," said the teacher. "It is through your study that you will gain wisdom."

So the young man piled the thousand and one books, some dry bread, and some candles on a cart. Then he took himself in cap and shawl, with paper in his shoes for warmth, to a small house at the edge of the town.

Inside the house, at the desk he sat, day after day, reading the thousand and one books. "Who am I?" he wrote on a paper.

"How am I connected to all others?" he wrote on a second.

Outside the trees turned fiery and lost their leaves. Inside, the young man filled page after page with learning from his books. He stopped only to swallow a little of the dry bread and sometimes to renew his candle or to drop his aching shoulders before him on the desk to sleep. The young man's wrists grew thin and his eyes burned. The thousand and one books stacked themselves around him in wobbly towers, and the pages of his writings heaped themselves before him like a fence.

One night a freezing rain beat in a torrent against the walls of the house. The young man pulled his shawl tight about him, but he felt the damp like a knife in his back. His feet were numb. The marks on the page before him began to swim. Suddenly the young man let out a moan and flung the book toward the window. "I don't know!" he yelled. "I DON'T KNOW!"

At that very second the rain outside halted and a howl of wind blew up. It clattered the panes and then, in a rush of power, ripped open the catch of the window. The room was filled with the shock of cold air. The candle blew out, and the papers on the desk spattered apart and lifted like the feathers of some giant white bird.

The young man staggered to the window and wrenched it shut. Then turning slowly and looking across the room, he drew back to see that a small light had formed on the other side of the swinging doors that led to the next room. "How can that be?" wondered the young man. "There is no one in this house but I."

The young man felt afraid. But the light glowed so softly. After a moment, the young man followed the glow to the other side of the doors. The pale light went on before him. This time he had to part a curtain to enter the next room. Still the glow went forward, and the young man found himself walking through room after room. He had not known the house had so many rooms. Was it possible he'd forgotten them? Had they been here before?

Finally the light drew him to a tightly closed door. He pushed it open, and the light settled on a bed in the small room.

The young man breathed out as he saw the light falter, then flare up, and then turn before his eyes into a beautiful woman. The woman's skin was dark and her hair curled about her face. Her garment was like the shadows of leaves. She looked quietly at the young man. The bed on which she sat was covered with quilts the color of shells. The walls seemed soft as clouds.

"Who are you?" whispered the young man.

"I am your soul," said the woman. "I am the Shekina. Eat and be full."

The woman turned and lifted to the bed a tray laden with a fruit. The young man felt ravenous. He fell to it and ate his fill.

The Shekina handed him a cup of steaming broth. The young man felt the warmth seep into his bones.

"Bathe now," said the Shekina.

Around him the young man could feel hot, lapping, washing water. Afterward a towel folded around him held in the sweet heat.

"Now. Come. Sleep," said the Shekina. She helped the young man into the bed.

For six days the young man clung to the Shekina, wrapped now in the deepest sleep, then awake and gazing into her eyes, and then holding her completely as he could. And then again drifting into the lovely heat of sleep.

On the seventh day, the Shekina kissed him deeply and rose up. Her skin then melted before him and he could no longer see her features. She faded again to a glow of light. The young man lay unable to move, his breath caught in his throat.

The young man didn't know how long he slept after that.

But the next time he opened his eyes, the sun was shining. He gathered up the pits of the fruits he'd eaten and went outside. There in the soil he planted a garden. At the center of the garden he placed a stone. On the stone he wrote these words:

"I am one with all. All is one."

Years passed by. The seeds of the fruits grew into a mighty orchard.

The young man was no longer young. Now he was an old man who carried his grandchildren.

Always on the seventh day, the old man lit the candles and whispered the story of the calling of the soul. "Come, Shekina," he would say to the breeze that flickered the candle flames bright. "Come, Shekina, come. Fill this garden with your rest."

Kuan Yin, Mother of Mercy

(kwan YIN)
China

Introduction

L ike the European mother of gods, whose worship as Mary, star of the sea, continues to this day against great institutional and theological odds, the great goddess of China survived the Buddhization of her realm by becoming Kuan Yin, mother of mercy. Often associated with the waters of the deep, perhaps riding a dolphin or a fish, Kuan Yin probably originated in the ancient Nu Kua, the great ocean-snail snake dragon woman who gave birth to all the life and the patterns of the universe (see story).

When Buddhism developed about 560 B.C.E., worship of the mother was already very old. Writers in 2000 B.C.E. exhorted readers to pray to the grandmother in a land already roamed by humans for a nearly unimaginable 496,000 years. While we do not know how many generations of people in those years revered the great feminine, we are almost certain that they recognized only their biological mothers, not their fathers. In such a setting, it is easy to imagine widespread awe for the female origins of life.

Buddhist storytellers, like their Greek counterparts who told of the goddess Athena's paternal birth (see story), said that Kuan Yin was actually a male who had reached a state of Buddha being and then decided to come to earth as a spiritual teacher in the form of a woman. By masculinizing her origins, and then placing her in a punitively male-dominated world, Eastern and Western tellers were undoubtedly trying to grapple with the reality of the great feminine in a patriarchal context.

Kuan means earth, and *yin* is the feminine balance to yang, both of which exist at the root of all the beings and workings of the world. *Yin* is a state and an energy that flows, creating gentle, consistent, and determined action.

Like Iamanja of Brazil (see story) and Mary (see story), Kuan Yin protects, relieves, and comforts in sorrow. She is related to the Japanese Kwannon, still worshipped in the Asakusa district of Tokyo. Her story is a retelling of the traditional one in Merlin Stone's *Ancient Mirrors of Womanhood*.

Because Kuan Yin is still as widely worshipped as Mary, her statue is easy to find. She, like Mary, can be called on for healing and mercy. I invoke her with willow branch or white flower floating in a bowl of water.

In the Land of the Dead

he goddess Kuan Yin longed to live among humans. Living so, she would understand the joys and sorrows of mortal life and increase her wisdom when humans called on her for help.

So one day Kuan Yin came to live as the youngest daughter of three in a house with a cruel father. When he didn't ignore his daughters, he spoke coldly to them. When they came of age, he raged. "I'm tired of you. Find yourselves husbands. Stay in their houses, not mine. You are not welcome here."

The eldest daughter married a silent warrior. The second wed a greedy merchant. But Kuan Yin said, "I do not wish to marry. I am going to live in the temple of the white bird with the lotus flowers in its fountain."

Kuan Yin went to live in the temple of the white bird with its roof of gold and black. When she continued to refuse to marry, her father arranged for the women in the temple to treat Kuan Yin harshly. "Make her do all the hardest work," he ordered. "Pull her hair. Give her only dry bread and water to eat. Then she will leave the temple and marry, as I command."

Some women at the temple were afraid, and they obeyed Kuan Yin's father. They gave her too much work and too little food. But, under the willow tree, Kuan Yin pretended to sleep, waiting until all the others slept. Then the green serpent came to help her carry the water. The white tiger appeared and gathered wood for the fire. The wrens busily collected vegetables from the garden. The spirit of the fire rose up and helped to cook the food. The peacock swept the kitchen floor with his thousand-eyed tail.

When Kuan Yin's father heard of the animals' help, he set fire to the temple. "Who dares defy me will die!" he roared.

But Kuan Yin put out the fire with her own hands and a branch from the willow tree. When her father saw that not only was the temple safe, but that the branch was not burnt, nor Kuan Yin's hands even blistered, his rage knew no bounds.

"Find her and cut off her head!" he ordered his servant.

The servant's sword, unable to harm the body of Kuan Yin, broke itself in two. But the servant, afraid to fail in the task of killing Kuan Yin, squeezed her throat with his hands until she could no longer breathe. Then he tied her lifeless body to the back of a yellow tiger, setting it loose in the jungle.

The land of the dead was dark, and Kuan Yin was afraid. But soon she sat up and began to sing. You know the songs she sang. The ones with the melodies that comfort and bring the sleep of renewal. The people who lived in the land of the dead gathered around Kuan Yin. They looked in wonder at her gentle face, and began to take each other's hands. They touched her soft robes, and began to chant and hum. Pain and loneliness melted into peace and joy.

The king of the dead was furious. "No singing in this place!" he thundered. "Begone!" And he banished Kuan Yin from the kingdom of death.

So Kuan Yin returned to earth and joined again her soul with her body. Floating and flying, she made her way to an island in the northeastern sea. There she lives to this day, chanting and singing for the well-being of all in the land of the living and the land of the dead. There, she puts out our fires with her sacred willow branch, and mercifully comforts us whenever we call out her name.

Sedna, the Great Woman at the Bottom of the Sea

(SAID-nuh)

Inuit

Introduction

S edna, also known as Arnaknagsak and Neqivik, has probably a dozen different names, depending on the language spoken in Greenland, Alaska, northern Canada, and the islands between. Sedna's country is the severe and beautiful land of the Inuit peoples, often called Eskimos by outsiders. Though a giver of life and abundance, her good is not to be worshipped: it is sufficient unto itself. Rather, her people vigilantly placate her that her power rest on the side of plenty and safety rather than barrenness and danger. Her people trust in the wisdom of her placaters, the medicine people and the storytellers—the *angakok*—for they are the seers who have touched the helping spirits with their souls.

Evil is real to the Inuit peoples. Daily they face great darkness, storms, gales, and stealthy fog. Despite the convenience of ready-made tools and electricity, the experience of generations shows that life is difficult: we humans constantly confront forces stronger than ourselves. Sedna embodies the innocence and the clarity, the evil and the good.

From her depths emanate the mysterious laws of life, which include the matter-of-fact necessity of death.

Depending on her pleasure, Sedna is the goddess who keeps back and sends out animals for the hunt, and to her she gathers all spirits who die of natural causes.

I have blended themes from more than one Inuit myth for Sedna's story. (See also story of Mayahuel.) This goddess helps me come to terms with sacrifice and with the tremendous shifts of life, so great that for the Inuit peoples they must be marked with an entire change of name. I invoke her with seawater and a wooden comb.

How the People Came
to Eat in Wintertime

he angakok are the special ones. They can converse with the sun and the moon. They travel to the underworld, going through rocks if need be. Indeed, the angakok know the way to the floor of the ocean. That is why they are able to tell the story of Sedna, the great woman who lives at the bottom of the sea. They tell of her before the change in her calling name, when she was young and lived only on the land. And they tell of her now, whose mercy and abundance we beg, soft and generous when we appease her by combing her flowing raven hair. Eyaya-eya!

In the old days, say the angakok, when the sun dogs never tired of pulling the sun across the sky, before humans came to earth, Sedna was the beautiful, flat-nosed land maiden called Avilayoq (a-VEE-luh-yoke.) Avilayoq lived among caribou, musk ox, reindeer, hare, fox, and the birds of the air. When Sedna was Avilayoq, say the angakok, the land knew only daytime. The goddess then, for centuries at a time, would beat the frame of her ayayut drum and croon the song of the land maiden. Handsome, free, and graceful was she: Eyaya-eya. Eyaya-eya.

Other times, she would sit on a rock, dressed in her most lovely clothes, quite still and staring out over land and sea, gazing for eons at the bottomless placid water that reflected the glowing colors of the sun hung red, yellow, and low in the sky. Silent and motionless, Avilayoq would drink in the rays of the sun broken into blue, green, and blinding white by the breaking, floating icebergs.

At other times, say the angakok, Avilayoq had the heart of a child at play with a ball. She skipped at the edge of the sea and teased the strong, persistent first sun dog, who lay his compliments so prettily at her enticingly booted feet. The day came, though, when Avilayoq saw that the eyes of first sun dog were flecked with kindness, and the tease in her heart turned to thrill.

Earth was never the same again, say the angakok, when Avilayoq took first dog as her husband. Avilayoq and sun dog built a snow hut to lie in, and the other sun dogs, leaderless now, rested in such a way that night came for the first time to the land of endless day. And out of the womb of Avilayoq came human beings: small and large of every age. They too began to make huts and to hunt for food on a land that was fast turning colder than Avilayoq had ever known before.

There had always been snow and ice, but now came an ominous thundering of that ice, louder than the beating of a thousand ayayuts. A violence of snow driving off the sea sent caribou and musk ox so deep into the freezing night that none could follow.

Gone was the laughter, the plenty, the sun. Come was the time of no eating, and the wails of her people filled the ears of Avilayoq. The heart of Avilayoq, say the angakok, grew heavy as a carcass. She wrung her hands for the fate of her humans. Then the picture of the quiet gazing of that endless summer filled her, and there was born in Avilayoq a plan that filled her both with peace and dread.

Avilayoq called her people to her. "You must gather the strength you have left," she called over the howling of the wind. "You must build a boat of skins. In that boat I will ride with the old man out into the sea. There will I calm this sky and call back the summer's food."

Weak as they were, the people were amazed. No one before had left the land for the waters. And to call back the summer's food! Eyaya-eya! Eyaya-eya!

The people built a boat of skins. Avilayoq dressed again in her finest clothes. To sun dog she said, "Life is heavier than death. It so happens that one is leaving."

"Are you leaving now?" asked sun dog, and though his eyes were filled with sorrow, he did not follow her.

Bent and falling, Avilayoq with the old man pulled themselves to the edge of the sea where the kayak waited tied to a bone stuck in the snow. Avilayoq and the old man climbed inside, and the old man cut the boat free with his axe.

The kayak rolled in the black waves like an eye in the head of a wounded caribou. The silhouette of Avilayoq stood tall, arms outstretched in the shrieking gray torrent. Avilayoq shouted, say the angakok. She begged the sky and the sea that had beckoned her so long ago.

But what happened next, say the angakok, is horrible to relate. No one knows why—some say it was a frenzy of terror—no one knows why, but the arms of the old man shoved. They shoved the land maiden into the pitching sea.

Avilayoq writhed against the icy cold that knifed her body. Her hands tore upward at the edge of the kayak, but the old man took up his axe and cut off the grasping fingers of the goddess.

With a terrible scream, the head of Avilayoq sank into the waters of the deep.

It was then, say the angakok, that the fine clothes of the land maiden slipped forever from her huge, beautiful body. Her hair, ripped from its hood, floated like wings about her. It was then that the severed fingers of Avilayoq changed to seals, to walrus, to polar bears, and whales. It was the body and blood of Avilayoq that gave the water animals to her people that they might hunt and eat also in wintertime.

It was then, say the angakok, that the land maiden, now the great woman of the sea, took the new calling name of Sedna. As Sedna, she lies at the bottom of the sea in her house like the houses of people. It is she we fear and she who gives forth all abundance.

But the thanklessness and broken promises of people, they say, collect like grease and dirt in her hair that her own hands are now unable to groom. It is by righting the wrongs of land and sea that we content her by running the comb of diligence, patience, and frugality through the sheets of her wild black hair.

IV

The Force of Life

Sexuality and Creativity

Desire turns the wheel of life on earth. Moon fancies the swell of the sea. Twilight waits, eyes soft, for the night. Birds nest again and again because they ache after flight. The artist speaks of having to create, of holding inside her something that she must express, the thing in her that leaps after life.

We give birth to ourselves over and over again. Before the birthings are the gestations. Before the gestations come the matings. Before the matings, the courtings and before them virginities. After the birthings, we grow, we lose, we mourn; we are babies all over again. Then, even as we cling to the breast, the cells in us bound after childhood.

Desire pulses at the center. In goddess consciousness, the sexual is sacred. In this ancient, new religion we are remaking together, worship means savoring, delighting, preserving, luxuriating. In goddess consciousness, we animate the field and the water as slyly and gratefully as we personify a lover's genital. In this religion, we indeed "follow our bliss," as historian of religion Joseph Campbell advised.

When sexuality is sacred, creativity—not compliance—is our attitude toward external reality. When we relate creatively and playfully to our worlds, we minimize the experience of feeling caught in someone else's mechanizations. Playing, creating, we are alive in space and time. Wishes and objects intersect. Whole spectra of feeling replace the sense of futility.

Sexuality now is far broader than feelings about reproductive functions or even purely pleasurable sexual acts or choices. Goddess sexuality is a metaphor for what we yearn for and to what we devote ourselves—not out of duty but rather ardor and zeal. Sexuality is the way we are intimate with our own feeling states; the way we are moved by the scent of eucalyptus on a rainy night walk; our paintings and letters; our laughter and stews; our persuasions and politics. Sexuality is our moment-by-moment, changing relish for who we are. Sexuality is our willingness to let ourselves really show in the world.

Even before the purposeful revival of goddess consciousness, people had begun to long for the kind of bodily state that would resacralize our beings. The "free love" and the drug culture of the late twentieth century were both mass attempts to break control-culture's bondage. But relaxed sexual mores and "being here now" in a culture that trashes earth with poisons and plastics and practices the "isms" of injustice only perpetuate the split between our bodies and earth; between our knowings and our beings. Other people and our own experiences are still objects to collect and consume. Our wielding of power over others and our finding ourselves in power-under positions, still make us slaves to what can be bought and taken. We find ourselves filled not with sacred feeling, but with the struggle to conceal from ourselves how much we have wasted and thrown away.

But the consciousness of the goddess is uncovering the waste. Over the chasm between our bodies and our souls, we are building a bridge of equal partnership between what we consume and what we nurture. In goddess consciousness we do not pretend that life contains no death. We honor the reality that the preservation of our own lives requires the deaths of plants and animals. We are frugal and mindful about our consumption. Nor do we pretend that death contains no life: we reuse and use again the endless cycle of our waste.

Furthermore, we are inventing new ways of relating the feminine to the masculine. Everywhere in nature are both forces. Nearly every kind of reproduction involves both the *yang* and the *yin*. Whether in homo-, hetero-, or autosexuality, we feel both masculine and feminine powers at work. We reject the oversized masculine of the control culture that has dominated our inner and outer lives. As the feminine comes into equal partnership within and without, we connect again with our souls, and our abilities to be human "beings" instead of human "doings," as psychologist and writer John Bradshaw has said.

In goddess mythologies, the great female often has a male consort. In the great circle of life, the consort or lover of the goddess, sometimes also her brother or son, is the edge and she is the center. He enters her sanctuary by invitation and with thanksgiving.

A sprained ankle and a cane helped me understand the goddess and her lover in my life. My ankle fat and purple, I found I existed, like the goddess, in majestic slowness. Like her consort, my cane was strong and available at my need; only together could we make the trip to the mail-box. Ancient and present in my body, supported and safe with my cane, I was not efficient, but I was alive. I watched a leaf fall and the clouds make gray gardens in the sky. Here was a partnership of feminine and masculine—the cane useless without me, my body needing its simple reliability.

Earth-centered spirituality, I am convinced, asks of us a similar part-nership. Our attitudes and technologies must be in service of the sacred well-being of the planet.

Huitaca, Queen of Pleasure

(whee-TAH-kah)
Chibcha

Introduction

L ike other original peoples of the Americas, the Chibcha of Colombia may have roots in northern Asia from which they are thought to have crossed the Bering Strait into Alaska as many as 42,000 years ago, reaching South America by 6000 B.C.E. The Chibcha worship the divine ancestress Bachue, whom they envision as both woman and snake. Bachue is teacher of peace and order and protector of agriculture for the Chibcha, a role similar to that of Isis, Demeter, and Lamia (see stories) for their peoples.

Like peoples the world over, the Chibcha picture the great mother in many ways. Huitaca is the aspect of the mother who is queen of love and pleasure. She is the owl moon woman, who cradles the rites of renewal and creation. The Chibcha pose her wisdom against that of the wandering Bochica, the masculine deity responsible for the teaching of spinning, weaving, and industry.

I wrote this myth for Huitaca in order to invoke the sense of "goddess time" that grows in lovely counterpoint to the production-oriented hustle of the city world in which I live. The hurried buying and selling for profit that the European-influenced world takes so for granted are hilarious (and tragic) distortions of human energy to peoples for whom earth is alive. Present day original peoples in Australia (the Australoids), for example, understand production in a completely different way than does the culture of control. The Australoids trade not for profit, but for symmetry. Goods are malign in and of themselves; they work against their possessors unless they are constantly in motion. Goods for the Australoids are tokens of intention: to trade, to meet again, to fix frontiers, to intermarry, to sing and dance, and to share ideas and resources. From this viewpoint, production of goods loses its tyranny and instead integrates into its rhythm personal, social, and spiritual well-being. Bruce Chatwin's *The Songlines* outlines this understanding of Australoid trade.

Huitaca, goddess of perfume and feasting, music and love, is certainly, for me, also goddess of the luxurious world that unfolds before me when I remove the clamp of the clock and listen, instead, to the lilt of my own bloodstream.

The Clock That
Was Really an Egg

n ancient times, the people of a certain village lived close to their goddess Huitaca. Always she was in their midst, and it was due to her presence that the people lived as if every day were someone's birthday, which, of course, it was. The people of the village worked hard. But if they were tired, they rested completely. If they were hungry, they ate. And they never made a bowl or a basket or a boat or a blanket without adding the finest colors and pictures they could imagine. The people strove to make the objects of their effort reflect the beauty of their goddess. So they sewed the birds and the sky onto their clothes, and grasses and rivers blew on their berry pots. When the people of the village lived close to Huitaca, they lived with feeling under their skins.

In those days, just anytime at all, the people made music. "Huitaca!" they called. "Come with bananas and bangles on your braids! Huitaca! Come dance with us!"

Then into reeds the people blew, and onto drums they beat. The seeds of gourds shook, shook, shook, and in color and singing the feet and bodies of the people stamped and swayed. Eyes shone and mouths drank dark pink juice and skins gleamed with sweat diamonds.

Huitaca whirled in the center fast as fire, and her chants spun men to men, men to women, women to each other, and back again the other way. Huitaca laughed and whooped and panted. Her people clapped and hugged and leapt.

Sometimes when the reed blowers slept and the fruits lay sucked dry near the spent honey-wine skin, Huitaca lay quiet with her people and looked at the sky. During the day, the villagers and their goddess found animals in the clouds. In the night, they cooled themselves under the scarves of shimmers that were the stars.

Huitaca was the bringer of perfume and play, jewelry and ornaments, soaps and oils, touching and love. When the people of the village lived close to Huitaca, they lived with feeling under their skins.

One day came the beginning of a big change in the village. Bochica arrived that day. Since he was a stranger—and a tall and strong one—the people gathered around him. Bochica had something the people had never seen before. It was small and round, with markings around the edge. "Is it an egg?" the people asked, touching the markings they thought were funny-shaped speckles. No, it was a clock, Bochica told them. He explained how the clock could measure out minutes and hours and days. "What's that good for?" the people wanted to know.

Bochica seemed surprised. "What's it good for?" he asked. "Why, without this clock, you can't make enough things to sell and buy."

"What's sell and buy?" asked the people.

Bochica shook his head. Now he seemed really surprised. "Look," he said. "You own a few things now, right?"

"Right," said the people.

"Well, if you had a lot more things, you could take them to the next village and get money for them, and with that money you can buy even more things!"

The people shook their heads this time. What strange ideas this Bochica had. "We have enough things," they said.

But they allowed Bochica to stay in the village with his clock and to make a home there. Every time the people called to their goddess Huitaca, Bochica shook his head. "Huitaca with her bangles and bananas," he muttered. "What good is all this music when there is work to do?"

Time passed, and Bochica continued to tell the people how fine it would be to sell and buy. For a long time, the people didn't listen to Bochica. "With Huitaca, we have all we need," they told him. "We're afraid your clock would make us forget that."

After a while, though, the people began to listen. They listened so much, in fact, that they did begin to forget Huitaca. They stopped putting oils and perfumes on their skins, and they didn't remember that every day was someone's birthday.

On the day the people decided to make Bochica their leader, Huitaca let out a cry. "Whoooooo?" she called out, and it sounded like a moan. When no one heard her, she turned herself into an owl and flew away.

No one noticed, except one little girl. "Mama, I saw Huitaca turn herself into an owl and fly into Bochica's egg," said the little girl to her mother.

"Shhhhh, child," said her mother. "Besides, that's a clock, not an egg."

"Bochica will make a fine leader," the people told each other. "He's tall and strong, and his clock will help us make enough things to sell and buy."

The people didn't know how the clock would help make things for them, but they soon found out. The clock told Bochica what time it was, and Bochica told the people when to work and when to stop and when to eat and when to sleep. Bochica walked all day among the people with his clock.

"That wall is taking too long," said Bochica. "Hurry up."

"But, Bochica, we're painting beautiful pictures on it," said the people.

"While you're wasting time on pictures," he said, "you could be making things to sell in the next village. Time to move on!"

Bochica thought that if every day is a birthday, that just means all the days are alike. "No need to have a party on an ordinary day, now, is there?" he said. "Too much work to do." And he strode by, telling people not to dawdle, to get busy, and to wake up.

Bochica never liked it either if someone made something he didn't know the name of. "We're making things to sell," he'd say. "Who's going to buy that thing, if they don't even know what it's called?"

Many years went by. For a long time people remembered when they had laughed and danced and made music. Sometimes they even tried to call Huitaca, just like in the old days. But she never came, and Bochica got angry if he heard them calling her or trying to make music. So after a while the only one who thought a lot about Huitaca was the little girl who'd seen her change into an owl. That little girl grew up and told her daughter the story. That daughter grew up and told her little girl the story.

By this time, too, Bochica was old. He looked pinched in the face and very thin. Late one hot afternoon, even Bochica got tired. "I'll sit down under this tree for just a minute," he said to himself. He carefully set his clock beside him and then fell asleep. Bochica began to snore.

A little girl picking berries nearby looked up when she heard Bochica snoring. She saw his clock beside him.

Now this was the very same little girl whose mother and grandmother had told her the story of Huitaca the Owl flying into the clock. So she wasn't at all surprised to find, when she crept very close, that the clock looked just like an egg. She touched it with one finger. The egg clock was warm and pretty. The little girl picked up the egg in both hands.

Certainly the little girl meant to take that clock to her mother, to show her how very much like an egg it looked. But in a second, the little girl had dropped that egg clock, and with a whirring of wings and a great "Whoooooooooo!" Huitaca herself flew out of the cracked pieces on the ground.

"Whoooooooo! Whoooooooo!" sounded Huitaca.

People were so busy they didn't notice at first. But the little girl began to run. "Huitaca! That's who!" she yelled.

"Huitaca!"

"Whoooooooo, whooooooo," said Huitaca as she circled above the village.

People began to look up from their work. Their spines began to tingle.

"Huitaca!" called the little girl. "Huitaca! It's your birthday!"

Then, just like in the old story her mother had told her, the girl called, "Huitaca! Come with bananas and bangles on your braids! Huitaca! Come dance with us!"

People stopped working. They looked at their hands and stretched their necks. They arched their backs and began to smile. People began to move. A man broke off a reed and began to blow it. Another turned over a pot and began to beat it. The seeds in gourds began to shake, shake, shake, and a ribbon of color and song began to form under the people's patting feet.

Bochica woke up. "My clock!" he cried out. He gathered the broken pieces to his chest. "Back to work!" he yelled. But no one heard in the swirl of music.

A chain of dancers pounded by, and the women scooped up the numbers from the clock to decorate their hair. The stars on the scarf of the sky began to sugar the night. With a great flapping of wings, Huitaca took woman form again, and her braids stood straight out as she whirled fast as fire at the center of her people.

After that night, the people of the village never again forgot Huitaca. They did not forget Bochica, either, with his selling and buying. But once again, they took the time they needed to reflect the beauty of their goddess in the things they made. No more work without making music. No more eating and sleeping only when it was time to eat and sleep. They ate when they were hungry and rested when they were tired. The people began to live again as if every day were someone's birthday, which, of course, it was. The people began to live again with feeling under their skins.

Athena, Mother of Invention

(uh-THEEN-uh)

Greece

Introduction

As Athena Parthenia, she who comes from herself, the holy virgin of Athens metamorphosed her form and name into the myths of an array of cultures. Like Lamia (see story), she rose up in the land the Greeks called Libya, what we know today as all of North Africa, except for Egypt. Called Neith, Anath, and Ath-enna, She was the triple goddess whose tremendous powers came to hold a special fascination for even patriarchal storytellers. Rather than obliterate her name, these tellers instead stripped from her the associations of moon, snake, and owl that encapsulated her woman mysteries. They invented the tale of her birth from the male god Zeus's head, and in dramas of war and strategy they dressed her in helmet and sword and placed in her mouth words that scorned women.

Misogyny could not obscure, however, the essence of clear-minded-ness that is Athena's special gift of fertility. Artist of real-world crafts, Athena, the great weaver, came to embody the complex skills of planning and follow-through in domestic and political arenas. Hers was the might of civilization itself.

I wrote this new myth for Athena in honor of plumbing, the stupendous, invisible weaving of pipes beneath every city, without which vast numbers of people living closely together cannot healthily function. As queen of sanitation engineering, Athena is similar to the Roman Cloaca, an aspect of Juno (see story), who was queen of sewers and excrement. Athena, called Minerva by the Romans, empress of architecture, is the goddess I call on to help me plan, edit, and organize. How important to discover that this realm, currently so split away from the feminine, actually originates with the mother.

The Weaving of the Streets and Plumbing

he goddess Athena got up in the morning and tied an apartment house onto each foot. She climbed into her skirt made of hospitals and libraries and pulled a shirt of towers over her head. She belted her waist and tied back her hair with two pillars. Into her pockets she stuffed streets and pipes.

Today was the day to finish her two great tapestries. Today in the cities, she would weave the last of her mighty threads. First she pulled the streets from her left pocket. Bending and turning, she poked and pressed them into the huge grid of roads she had made.

Then she walked down into the earth. There gleamed the net of pipes she had strung down the walls of the buildings, under the halls, past the steel and brick foundations. From every tub, every sink, and every toilet angled the pipes, curving and pointing out to the sea. Under the earth, Athena squatted. Using the last of the pipes from her right pocket, she measured, sawed, and screwed them until they fit just so.

The people had gathered. Hundreds waited on foot and with carts at the sides of her roads. Hundreds waited at the edge of the sea beside the huge vats that would catch the waters of Athena's pipe weaving. Hundreds stood high on the mountain where the waters began.

Athena climbed out of the earth and stood at the center of the cities where all could see her. She loosed the pillar from her hair, and a rush of air lifted the mass of it and settled it into the clouds.

"It is finished!" Athena shouted. "My tapestries are finished!"

The people cheered.

"Now hear the story of my tapestries," said Athena.

The people listened.

"My roads I call my transportation tapestry," said Athena. Her voice was loud and strong. "Without the streets of my tapestry, your travel is clumsy and long. With my streets, your travel is easy. With my streets, your travel is free of rocks and thorns. When you visit and work or gather and carry, you go straight and true to each other."

The people waved branches and raised their voices. They tossed flowers by the thousands into Athena's great transportation tapestry.

Athena spoke again. "I call my pipe tapestry plumbing," she said. "My plumbing carries away your wastes and your filth. Without my plumbing your cities stink and are full of disease. With my plumbing, your cities are clean and your air fresh."

The people clamored at their beautiful Athena. They called her name and cheered. Then the man who stood at the great spigot at the top of the mountain waved a white cloth high.

"We are ready, Athena!" the man yelled. He raised his huge hammer. "We are ready to start the waters flowing in your great plumbing tapestry!"

"Wait!" thundered Athena. "You are not ready!"

The people stirred. They looked at each other. The man at the spigot lowered his hammer.

Athena held out her hands. "My people," she said. "You have not heard the end of my story."

The people waited.

"Today," said Athena, "you are grateful for my gifts to you. Today you fill my roads with flowers. Today you sing the praises of Athena, the great street maker and plumber."

"But," she rumbled, "there will come a time when you will forget. There will come a day when you will forget that your roads and your plumbing are mine. There will come a day when you will want to abuse my weavings."

The people raised their voices in disbelief.

"Quiet!" said Athena. Then her shoulders drooped. But her voice was still strong. "There will come a day, my children, when you will build fast machines that spew out poison into the air over my roads. You will dump poison at my roadsides. There will come a day, my children, when you will pour poison into my plumbing. 'We can't see it,' you will say. 'So what does it matter?' That is the day you will forget to clean the waters of my plumbing before they pour into the sea."

Athena hung her head. The people were silent. They shook their heads. They could not imagine forgetting the great weaver or her gifts. Then a woman cried out, "Athena! We will not forget."

Athena lifted her head. The people took up the cry. "Athena! We will not forget!" they shouted. "We will tell our children. And our children will tell their grandchildren."

Athena's shoulders straightened. She took two steps, and the earth shook under her weight. She stretched out her arms and cupped her left hand around the people on the mountain. She cupped her right hand about the people at the edge of the sea. The people at the sides of her roads pressed together.

"My children," said Athena, and her voice was like a thousand harp strings. "See that you do not forget. See that you do not forget that the tapestries are mine."

"Never!" cried the people. "We will never forget!"

Athena smiled. "Then we are ready," she said. "Turn the faucet!"

The man at the spigot on the mountain threw his whole weight into the hammer blow that turned the giant faucet. Again and again he hammered, and then the water began to flow. A trickle at first and then a roar of white and blue filled the coppers and silvers of Athena's great plumbing tapestry.

The people began to dance in Athena's streets. Athena held her fists in the air. Inside the buildings, the sounds of flushing and splashing gurgled forth. Dishes sparkled and babies patted hands into warm baths. "Never forget, never forget," patted the babies' hands.

Outside the buildings, the carts moved to and fro on the crisscross streets. "Never forget," squeaked the axles. "Never forget," fluttered the birds.

"Never forget," hummed the people at the vats at the edge of the sea.

"Never forget," dreamed the waves and the fishes and the long green hair of the plants at the bottom of the sea.

Bridget, Inventor of Writing

(BRIDGE-it)

Ireland

Introduction

Impossible to banish, the great goddess Danu (see story) later took the human-divine form of the goddess Bridget and finally accepted the status of "sainthood," conferred on her by Pope Gregory I. The pope told Augustine in the sixth century C.E. to co-opt rather than destroy the pagan sites and customs of the newly evangelized Celtic peoples. The church thus added the new Saint Bridget to the nativity scene, calling her midwife to the Virgin Mary. They changed the name of her holy Imbolg, February 1, to Candlemas, only thinly disguising with the trappings of Christianity its pagan reverence for the union of light and land.

But Irish writers, refusing to diabolize their goddess or even fully to accept her "sainthood," insisted on calling her Queen of Heaven, and they identified her with the Christian mother of God. Certainly their Bridget, triple goddess of the Celtic empire of Brigantia, which included parts of the British Isles, Spain, and France, was once known as mother of all life. Identified with the changing moon and associated with the ox (a later nativity scene prop), boar, and ram, Bridget also personified the entire kingdom. She conferred prosperity on a king only when she ritually accepted him as her spouse. Her sacred count was nineteen, the number of years it takes for the new moon to coincide with the sun's winter solstice. Her priestesses, too, numbered nineteen; for centuries their generations kept her sacred fire burning in Kildare, Ireland.

To this day, the custom of fashioning Bridget's cross is widespread. In honor of her fertility, people in the Gaelic-rooted parts of the isles weave, of rushes or straw, three- or four-armed crosses on the first day of spring, the time of preparation for the first planting. Though its precise meaning is lost in antiquity, the cross may well symbolize the sacred union of the powers above and below.

Adored of poets and giver of medicine, smithcraft, and writing, Bridget, queen earth herself, wears the cloak of Catholicism with regal nonchalance. Her story is adapted from the one told in *Ancient Mirrors of Womanhood* by Merlin Stone.

I call on Bridget on February first or second when the first yellow-flowered sourgrass has burst through the ground after winter rains. Then I set in earth a new plant in honor of the project or quality I have resolved to grow in my life this next year. I feel Bridget's presence when I, mid-month, drink two cups of that surprisingly cheap, easily-acquired mugwort tea which brings blood cramplessly and obliterates the need for painkillers.

Queen of the Four Fires

long time ago, near the beginning, at the first crack of pink in a young morning, near the waters of the magic well, the goddess Bridget slipped into the world and the waiting hands of the nine sisters who swayed and crooned in a great circle around her. The waters of the magic well burbled their joy.

Up rose a column of fire out of the new goddess's head that burned to the very sky. Bridget reached up her two hands and broke away a flaming plume from her crown of fire and dropped it on the ground before her. There it leapt and shone, making the hearth of the house of the goddess.

Then from the fire of her hearth, Bridget used both hands to draw out a leaping tongue of heat, swallowed it, and felt the fire burn straight to her heart. There stood the goddess, fire crowning her head, licking up inside her heart, glowing and shooting from her hands, and dancing on the hearth before her.

The nine sisters hummed and the waters of the magic well trembled as Bridget built a chimney of brick about her hearth. Then about the chimney, she built a roof of thatch and walls of stone. And so it was that by the waters of the magic well the goddess finished the house in which she keeps the four fires which have served her people forevermore.

Out of the fire on Bridget's hands baked the craft of bending iron. Out of the fire on Bridget's hearth and the waters of her magic well came the healing teas. Out of the fire on Bridget's head flared out writing and poetry. Out of the fire in Bridget's heart spread the heat of compassion.

Word of the gifts of Bridget's fires traveled wide. People flocked to learn from Bridget the secret of using fire to soften iron and bend it to the shapes of their desires. The people called bending iron smithcraft, and they made wheels, pots, and tools that did not break.

All the medicine plants of the earth gathered in the house of the goddess. With their leaves, flowers, barks, and roots, and the waters of her magic well, Bridget made the healing teas. She gave a boy with weak teeth the tea of the dandelion root. She gave a young woman the tea of the raspberry leaf to help her womb carry its child. An old man, a cane in each hand to help him walk, took from Bridget wintergreen bark for his pain and black cherry juice for the rheumatism. She gave comfrey to a girl with a broken leg and blue cohosh to bring her bloods without cramps. Bridget brewed motherwort, licorice root, and dried parsley for a woman who was coming to the end of her monthly bleeding. "Cup a day," said Bridget, "that you stay supple and strong."

The people wanted Bridget's recipes. "But we can't remember which plants for which healings, where to gather them or how long to steep them," they told Bridget.

The fire on Bridget's head blazed bright. She took up a blackened stick and made marks with it on a flat piece of bark. "These are the talking marks," she said. "They are the way to remember what you don't want to forget."

The talking marks also let the people write down the stories of her wisdom.

Once two men with the terrible sores of leprosy came to Bridget.

"Bathe yourself in my well," said Bridget to the first man. At every place Bridget's waters touched, the man's skin turned whole again.

"Now bathe your friend," said Bridget.

Repulsed, the man backed away from his friend. "I cannot touch him," he said.

"Then you are not truly healed," said the goddess. And she gave the first man back his leprosy and healed the second man. "Return to me with compassion," she said to the first man. "There find your healing."

Every year at midwinter the people thank Bridget for her well of wisdom and her fires of hand, hearth, head, and heart. "Thank you, Bridget, for the smithcraft, for the healing teas, the talking marks, and compassion. May you dwell with your fires in your house by the waters of your magic well forevermore."

Shakti, Queen of the Cosmos

(SHOCK-tee)

Hindu

Introduction

The goddess Shakti's name translates as "cosmic energy." In Hinduism, she is the dominant force of the universe. (See stories of Devi, Maya, and Kali, other forms of the Shakti.) She alone has the power to move the dormant male force to action, and a god without his Shakti is helpless. The Shakti is time, the cosmic tension and activity that brings the corpse of eternity to life over and over again. Shiva, her consort, is that eternal dancer who comes to life in her arms. It is in relationship to her that the god Shiva expresses the essence of his character. He creates, maintains, destroys, conceals, and favors, all at her will, multiplying himself into endless actors, like vapor, coming to pass, to flow, and to vanish.

Tantric Hinduism worships the sexual principle as a metaphor for life itself. Life's energies of water, earth, and snake are embodied by the Shakti's *yoni,* or sacred vulva. The Shiva's *lingam,* or sacred phallus, embodies the energies of fire, sun, and eagle. As in the Central American goddess Mayahuel's relationship to Snake-the-Wind (see story), this mythology poses none of the West's opposition between snake and sun (devil and god), but instead honors the union of differences as the ultimate power of the universe.

The Shakti and her Shiva together dance at the center of the universe. This center is within each human heart. The western mystical system called alchemy, which concerns itself with the substance and transformation of the soul, honors this same heart center, and uses extensive sexual imagery. The chant *OM* or *AUM,* made popular in the United States by students of the East in the 1960s and 1970s, recapitulates the spectrum of worldly states represented by the Tantric goddess and her consort. *A* is the state of waking consciousness in the world of gross experience. *U* is the state of dreaming consciousness. *M* is the state of dreamless, blissful sleep, undifferentiated nonexperience. The pause of silence that follows *AUM* is the ultimate un-manifestation of divine reality.

The dance of the god Shiva is far better known than the inspiration of his Shakti. Discovering the Shakti has given me great satisfaction. I wrote the story of the Shakti in order to invoke the tremendously private feeling I have about these two cosmic forces.

The Shakti and the Shiva
at the Center
of the Human Heart

 take my sister. I take my son. I take my
lover. I take my friend. But in the end I
have to go alone to the center of my heart.

At first I said, let's not waste time. And
anyway I am afraid. I want a hand to hold.

But I have to go alone. I go alone, I'm telling you. Yet when I get to
the center, I am not alone. For the Shakti and her Shiva are there.

Past the teachings and the wishings I go, under the corrections and
the rules. I move through the kaleidoscope of my world. The wind
brushes my ears; the sun colors me hot. The rains come. I travel past
the jeweled elephants and the purple curtains of principles and politics. I turn through the spiral of peacocks and calves, under the castle entwined with roses and long green rice. I swim under the fan of
the lotus into the warm black mud of the roots. I float. I float down
to the deep. The silence there is like a cape. I can feel the eye in my

mind close in peace, and I sing the song of nothing without any words.

Then I hear the sound of *aaaaa* around me. The eye in my mind darts open. I can see I've come to a red velvet room. Inside stands a bed hung with silk. But I can not go in, for two black tigers pace its entrance. Two black tigers—one striped yellow and the other white. I recoil. I wish for my friend. I press away and the sound of *aaaaa* presses back on me. I see the mouths of the tigers yawn. Their teeth and scalloped lips glint wet.

I snap shut the eye in my mind. The sound of *uuuuu* comes to me. When I open that eye again, behold! The tigers, first the yellow, then the white, scratch their spines against the floor, forepaws limp with pleasure, the fur of their bellies rumpled and soft. That sound of *uuuuu* clasps me tight, and I am able now to enter the room. There the Shakti and her Shiva hold each other on the flower-strewn bed.

I am shy. Surely this embrace is not meant for my eyes. But I stare. The blue blacks of their heads look like rocks in a moving river. I feel the sweeping longing and fascination of a child. Oh! I know I must go.

But the Shiva sits up. "Stay!" he says. The movements of his chest and wrist are graceful as a cat's.

"This is the center of your heart, after all," says the Shakti. Her eyes are laughing, and she's hooked a hand over the rosy blanket at her neck. "Stay and let us tell you our story."

Shiva pats the bed and inclines a welcome with his eyes and chin.

I hold my breath.

"Come," says the Shakti. Her arms reach out to me.

I scramble.

And there I am between them smelling their jasmine and patchouli, enveloped like a yolk in an egg. The sound of *mmmmm* swells around me—*mmmmm*—and I sleep.

When I awake, I trace with my finger the design imprinted on my forearm by the cuddle of covers. There, while I lie tiny between them, they tell me their story.

"At the beginning of every beginning," says the Shakti, "I am alone.

There is nothing. I am like a windless red flag, vibrant with color but not moving. And I watch my lord Shiva. The lashes on his cheeks are so pointed and fine. His cheeks are like wax. He is so still, then. So unbelievably still."

"She says I look dead," says the Shiva.

"You do, you look dead. There is nothing. So I drift and I float. I lie with myself and I dream," says the Shakti.

"And then, finally, she wakes me," says the Shiva.

"Yes, I want him up! I want a breeze in my flag. So I kiss him. I wake him up with my kisses."

The Shakti and her Shiva lace their fingers over me. I feel so safe that I wiggle.

"Oh, how you wake me, my queen," says the Shiva.

"I wake him for the dance," says the Shakti. "And how you dance, my lord! Oh! You can dance!"

I turn my face up to the Shakti's. Her eyes looking over me to her Shiva are melting.

I see the Shiva's mouth and eyes, too, soft and wet. He turns his head down to mine and draws his finger across my forehead. "You can imagine the dance," he says.

I feel a knowing, an excitement. Oh, I can imagine that dance! Shiva turns his wrists and buildings hoist to the sky. Shiva's foot arches and lovers cling. His knees unfold and with his leap monies glitter through the chutes of the marketplace. With the undulation of his back can come war and pestilence; his chest might ripple and a library rise and fall. The skin of his cheek might stretch taut and the new year's crop burst with fruit. At the flicker of his tongue, the dying hold the living; at the flinging of his arms, the quake erases a nation.

Like a drop of his sweat, my life might roll like a cat in the sun, purring, then springing after its prey. In a race down his side, my life could realize its promise. Caught in the crease of his elbow, it might lie still. One day it would evaporate into the air he would breathe again.

I feel the knowing, the excitement. Oh, yes, I can imagine this dance!

The Shakti and her Shiva curl their arms about me in the nest of their heat. The lips of the Shakti are reddened and full.

"Your limbs and your contours!" says the Shakti to the Shiva. "You are like a melody."

"And you the breath that sings me, Beloved," says the Shiva.

The room mutes around me. And I sleep again. But this time I dream. The shapes of the queen and her lord are subtle now. They fade in and out. First she is enormous and the Shiva but her finger's width. Then they are fighting. Can it be? They speak harshly, and I cannot see her face. Then he chases, frantic and alone. Now she appears again, like the mother to the child crying after the nightmare. Now her face is one of ecstasy: she collects to her throbbing triangle of life his magnificent flowering tree of desire. Oh! How the picture blazes and fades in that dark and fiery place!

I am spinning then. Turning past the velvet and the tigers, into the floating peace of nothing and then the *aum* sound all around me. Past the mud and the roots, up between the fan of the lotus and over the castle entwined with roses and the long green rice. I sift through the spiral of calves and peacocks, past the jeweled elephants and the curtains of principles and politics. Back through the rain and the sun and the wind.

I am back with you now, my daughter, my brother. I am back with you now, my lover, my friend. Back from the center of delight and pain. Up from the shades of death and the elixir of immortality. Up from the everlasting temple of the Shakti and her Shiva. Up from the center of my heart and the secret of the world.

Mary, Queen of Heaven

Europe

Introduction

The queen of heaven in the person of Mary has been so minimized that anger and pain have often outweighed my ability to connect with her as goddess. Indeed, through the ages, male church leaders have wrestled to stuff the love for the mother they could not rid from their congregations into the box of Virgin Mother, shutting from common cultural understanding the sacredness of full sexuality. Arguments about her "history" have raged: church fathers have periodically attempted to prove her neither divine nor maternal. But in the first centuries of the church's existence, leaders saw that without the worship of this combined Stella Maris, Juno, and Mariamne, ancient spinner of fate, and begetter of savior, their institution was doomed. Gothic cathedrals were regularly built over shrines to the originator goddess and dedicated to "Our Lady," or Notre Dame, becoming truly palaces for the queen of heaven. Ambivalence born of denial and ignorance continues to this day: recently a Jesuit priest enthusiastically touted the inspiring new theory that Mary, in agreeing to birth Jesus, was really the first disciple of Christ.

Like most people in modern culture, my first experience with the goddess, unbeknownst to me, was with Mary. Raised as a Protestant rather than a Catholic, I met her when I was seventeen in Mexico in the purple velvet, candlelit churches of Sinaloa. The sensuality and warmth of those rooms greatly comforted me; after the spare, ascetic sanctuaries of my childhood in which the spirit was the bodiless word, these female-filled chapels washed me with relief.

I recently called on Mary at an afternoon mass in the Catholic church near the graveyard of my Protestant ancestors in southwest Ireland. While the elderly congregation chanted, "Hail, Mary, full of grace, the Lord is with thee; blessed art thou among women and blessed is the fruit of thy womb, Jesus; Holy Mary, Mother of God, pray for us sinners now, and at the hour of our deaths," I too softly chanted a prayer to the Star Goddess, borrowed from the traditional one that encodes her own words: "Hail, Mary, full of grace, the dust of whose feet are the hosts of heaven; you are the white moon among the stars and the desire of human hearts; you are the mystery: that if that which we seek we find not within, we will never find it without; for you were here at the beginning and you are that which is attained at the end of desire."

Challenged by friends to write the Christmas story from Mary's point of view, I came to terms with her story as an extension of both the ancient story of Mayahuel and her Fish Son and the Roman story of Juno as the yearly creator of light (see stories). My inspiration for Mary's story comes from the famous *Vierge Ouvrante,* a statue depicting the familiar, gentle Madonna and Child, whose opened hinges reveal inside her: God, Jesus, the angels, and the saints of heaven.

Mary and
the Birth of Light

n the midst of the darkness, Mary, Queen of Heaven, opened the flower at her center. Gently, slowly, in the midst of the darkness, she opened herself, breathing a sugar of stars into the silent night. Softly, tenderly, she spread the brown petals under the tips of her gathering hands. In the midst of the night, in the glitter of stars, Mary dreamed and touched her flower moist in the darkness.

In the midst of the darkness, the flower of Mary heated and swelled. In the starry, breathing night, the fingers of Mary grew firm and sure and the flower's edges melted into the center. Into circles it melted, and out of the center came a cave in the shape of a stable: a box of warm breathing in the midst of the night. Out of herself, to surround her, birthed the Queen of Heaven a cave: simple, humble, thick-smelling, dark, and deep under the night of the sky.

In the midst of the darkness, Mary's hands cradled her flower. In the midst of the night, the cave cradled its queen. In the midst of the cradle, in the midst of the circles, in the midst of the gathering, her breath became music. Out of the music, out of the scent, out of the body of the Queen of Heaven came the animals of magic. Out of the breathing, out of the waves, out of the pliable, bending night came the animals that filled her cave with their heat and their help.

Out of Mary's knees came the donkey. Shaggy, brown, carrier of burden, keeper of patience. Out of the knees of the queen came the donkey, filling the cave with intractable certainty.

Out of the breasts of the queen came the cow. White and red, milk and blood; cycles of pondering; enduring; full, placid heat in the stable of holiness.

Out of the feet of the queen came the sheep. Simple and following, bleating their needs.

And when the music of holiness touched the rafters of the stable, the dove and its mate flew from her arched-back throat.

There in the dark, there in the shuffling heat, there in the cave song of the Queen of Heaven, there made the animals the nest for the light to come.

Then from the eyes of the Queen of Heaven rose up the beloved husband. Husband with the long hard back. Husband with the kissing hands. Husband to lie with, searching, rejoicing. Husband to enwrap and to touch again the flower at her center. To have and to hold, the Queen of Heaven birthed the beloved husband.

Then, out of the swelling, out of the thick, heavy, coiling dark, out of the belly of the Queen of Heaven, out of her, slipping and searing, into the soothing of the beloved husband, into the dark of the stable, into the giant night, slid the Sun of the World.

Out of the body of Mary came the Son of Light. There at her breast he slept, while the beloved husband smoothed back the Queen of Heaven's hair. There slept the child, filling the stable with light. There moved the animals. There slipped the tears down the face of the queen.

There in the night glowed the new light of the world, precious, whole, and alive at the center.

And it came to pass that the night was filled with multitudes of heavenly hosts praising her name and crying hosannah to the highest and the lowest and all the bleating, mewing worlds that lay between.

Baubo, Ancient Face
of Demeter and Persephone

(BOW-bo)

Greece

Introduction

I n an alternate telling of the Demeter and Persephone myth (see story), Baubo the crone dances erotically for Demeter, causing her to laugh. Demeter's laughter encourages Helios the sun to emerge from his seclusion (where he, too, mourns his lost child, Phaethon). Persephone then begins her ascent from the underworld. In a similar role, Ame-no-Uzume, another old woman, dances erotically for the Japanese Amaterasu Omikami.

An ancient Greek artist carved Baubo simply as a face on the pubic triangle above a woman's legs. Baubo is the personification of a paneroticism, born of delight for body and earth. Accustomed to the automatic desexualization of old women, to the grotesque witches of fairy tales, we are left first wide-eyed and breath-held by Baubo and her dance. Could we? Can we? Mother may we? (See stories of Hecate and Spider Grandmother.) Baubo is the erotic we have hidden away. She is she who marries herself. She is the caring daring that wakes up the world.

Baubo's Dance

nce upon a time, the earth dressed all the year in tendriling green. Helios the sun rose early every morning and delayed his bedtime as long as possible to be able to talk and laugh with the two great goddesses below. Demeter, queen of all green, and her fawn-eyed daughter, Persephone, played in an endless spring and summer.

But one terrible day, Persephone was stolen underground. Demeter mourned. Helios hid himself away. Fall and winter came to the land. Demeter searched for her daughter and found Baubo instead. Because of Baubo, Demeter laughed and Helios shone again. Only then was Persephone able to return to the upperworld.

It happened like this.

One day Persephone said good-bye to Demeter. The girl's lips felt like petals on her mother's cheek. "Be careful," said Demeter, without knowing why. There should be no danger, after all, for goddesses in an endless spring and summer. But a strange fear stabbed Demeter's heart.

"I will, Mama, I will," said Persephone, and she skipped away. Demeter watched her lickety-split the meadow until she was only a mark in the distance.

Persephone wandered. She fingered the skirts of the poppies that blew in the bee-buzzed grasses. She scattered dandelion tufts. Farther away, she drank from a pond and studied with solemn eyes her face in its cool black mirror. With her fingertips, she touched her full lips. She lowered and raised her lashes. She stroked her neck for a moment, then left off, sighing. Then, she gazed for a long time at something beneath her face in the pool. Finally, she dreamed against a hot red rock while the scent of narcissus rose thick around her.

Suddenly before her was a man on a horse. The animal's nostrils distended over its soft mouth, and the black-garbed man swung himself down to talk to the startled girl. From the center of the earth, he said he'd come. Wondering, intrigued, now coy, she listened. His words relaxed her, then began to probe. Her breath grew eager and she felt her pulses come alive.

Demeter saw none of this. She heard only the scream. When she rushed to look for her child, she found only a crumpled shoe next to the giant red rock. The grass around it was trampled as though there had been a struggle. Demeter could find her daughter nowhere, and Persephone did not come home. It was Helios who told her that Persephone had been stolen away by Hades to his underworld. The fear in Demeter's heart changed to terror. Helios, remembering his own lost child, turned away in sorrow.

Demeter could not stop hearing her daughter's scream. The next morning she could not move. Helios had to struggle to get out of bed. Darkened days stuttered by, and the world withered without the attention of the queen of all green and of Helios the sun. Trees lost their leaves, wheat and barley shriveled on the stalk, fruits withered and shrunk away to dry pits. Helios hid himself, and snow covered everything but old Baubo's house. Baubo, friend of the animals, baked, spun, and sipped tea in her house nestled in a valley.

The animals, not wanting to starve, began a trek to Baubo's house. They scurried, scuttled, and shivered. They clambered in and out of the deep white drifts.

Baubo opened her house to them all.

Finally, even in the dark, Demeter found her way to Baubo's house in the valley. By the glow of its windows, she could see the tangle of anise and roses on the roof; she could smell vanilla orchids fermenting at its windows. Suddenly, a gust of warm purple air billowed and lifted Demeter, tattered and spattered with mud, all the way to the latch.

The door swung open. Inside, from a room lit with beeswax tapers, a skinny, old woman offered her an apple.

"I am Baubo, pretty one," she rasped, "and this is for you."

The old woman's breath smelled of anise and vanilla. Her breasts hung low in her blouse; her irises, frosted white, glowed. Hairs bristled on her chin.

Demeter did not take the apple, but allowed herself to be steadied over the doorsill. Baubo put the apple on the plank of the table. Demeter sat stupefied on a stool, swaddled by the yeasty steam drifting from the belly of a black oven. Baubo fed her porridge. Sitting in a chair, she watched Demeter spoon it as a child would, not caring for the drips. Cupboards and a bed piled with quilts and round pillows hulked in the shadows.

Finally, Demeter wiped her mouth on her sleeve and looked up.

"It's time to talk," said the old woman.

Demeter put her daughter's shoe on the table. She fidgeted with its edges, then began to cry quietly. She told about the good-bye, the scream, the matted grass at the side of the red rock, about Persephone's not coming back. She told how the sun had gone away, how the ice and snow had come, how she had traveled here to this house in the valley.

Baubo's mouth had been still as she listened. Now it twitched. She reached for the shoe. Muttering with effort, she drew from the cavern of its toe a knife. The blade glinted in the candle flames. Knife and shoe now lay on the table next to the apple.

Demeter's eyes widened. She searched Baubo's face.

Then out of the corners, out of the cupboards, creeping from under the bed, came a wild, alive hatching of the whole room. Three swallows swooped from the rafters. A beaver bared her teeth and slapped her tail beside a bucket. A weasel nosed open the lower shelf of a cupboard. Four squirrels chattered on the windowsill. The pillows on the bed uncurled as serpents, hissing and curving from side to side. Animals rose up everywhere and a music began. A mole shuffled. Two deer clacked antlers. Six rabbits thumped. Three starlings cackled. From behind the bed, a wolf pointed her nose to the ceiling and bayed. A bear stamped back and forth before the black-bellied stove. A cluster of bees swarmed overhead.

Baubo wagged her head and peppered the table with her fingers and palms. She pushed herself up. She cut her eyes at the bear. She patted her feet. She flicked her skirt at the fox. She parted her blouse for a mink. Slowly, hair, breasts, and limbs undulating, Baubo began to dance.

The animals drummed.

Baubo swayed her hips. She picked up her feet. She showed her back, turned her front. Sweat beaded her lip.

With a flicker of the first hope she'd felt in weeks, Demeter stood up.

Baubo shrugged away her blouse. The rhythm climbed. Baubo whirled and with one hand gathered her skirts to her waist. A scar showed purple on her belly.

Baubo twirled and arched her neck.

Demeter's lips parted.

Baubo danced her thighs open and touched the wisps of the hair between her legs. She closed her teeth over her lower lip, flirted her eyes at Demeter, and humped.

Demeter laughed.

Baubo chortled.

Demeter snatched up the knife, splitting the apple into two creamy, starred halves. Then she slit the rags from her body. The knife clattered to the floor, and she reached for the hand of the hag. Their two hands seized, and the house in the valley sobbed with sound.

Away in the distance, Helios shook his head, not sure if he'd heard correctly. The music swelled and Helios nodded, wonder and hope in his heart. He stepped to his door.

Inside the house in the valley, Baubo and Demeter whooped.

Helios smiled. Then he walked into the sky.

Sunlight peeked in through the windows of the house in the valley. It glanced off the brown apple seeds. It lit the bear's wet snout and shivered in the mole's whiskers.

Down the road, icicles cracked loudly on tree branches and broke away.

Then a huge red rock above the valley trembled as if someone were heaving it aside from underneath.

V

Surrender

I 've spent a lot of my life identifying with my will and avoiding any activity I've thought smacked of the loss of it. Surrender, I was sure, was a word about conquering myself and others. Surrender couldn't possibly have anything to do with my juicy, flowing goddess.

Since surrender to what-is seemed tantamount to loss of self, I, early on, without knowing it, began to manipulate my perception of facts. I created my own personal control culture. I disregarded real information about myself and the world if it did not fit how I thought it should be. I simplified; called facts either black or white. I became quietly, determinedly obsessive about my efforts to change people, things, and even places to fit my visions. My attitudes were, in turn, manipulated by my willfulness. I was anxious and unreasonable without knowing it. I became so unaware and unaccepting of my own feeling states that I could not imagine believing that my own real needs and wants might be the beginning of a conversation between myself and this palpable changing being-ness I call goddess.

But I've come to understand that surrender isn't necessarily about war, rape, and personal invisibility. It's not about buckling to the thing I loathe to prove my piety. I've come to believe that surrender in goddess consciousness is about admitting my limitedness relative to her pervasive power. The order that I cannot know, I've come to call her. In relationship to the goddess, I've come to understand that surrender is the relinquishment of my childhood-based certainty that I can and must force the facts to be different.

Strangely, when I live with ambiguity and my own relative helplessness in the context of this order that I cannot know, I gain a clarity and peace about my actions that I never had when I poured my energy into trying to order my world. Goddess mirrors the states of a world in which everything, including myself, flutters out of reach of my butterfly net and silver pins. The truth is that I love and hate inconveniently; I get tired when I'm supposed to be performing; friends have feelings that dash my expectations; and my behavior disappoints others when it pleases me. I get angry; I get sick; grief does not clear up like a cold.

As I now understand it, surrender neither degrades nor requires the submission of one person to another. It's about bending to the truths of womb and tomb; to the murky, contradictory truths of body, partnership, and planet. Surrender is accepting; opening my deepest bodymind to the endless shifts of existence.

Sun Woman

Arunta

Introduction

Before the European Caucasians began to force themselves onto the continent of Australia two centuries ago, the aboriginals, who prefer to be called Australoids, were the land's original peoples. Then they numbered five hundred tribes and three hundred thousand individuals. Today they are only forty thousand and have been largely pushed out of the fertile eastern sections of the continent onto the deserts of the central regions.

The Australoid peoples tell the stories of the ancients who lived under the world and came out at the beginning to sing into being the rivers, the ranges, the salt pan, and the sand dunes. The ancients wrapped the world in a web of song, a net of music trails that even today enliven the land's forms and inhabitants, though the colonizer may be deaf to the sacred sound. Their song sung, the ancients went back to the cave holes that bore them, leaving the records of these wondrous cantatas on wooden and stone *churingas* (record sticks) for the people, to be guarded by every generation forevermore.

Yhi is the Sun Woman of the Arunta people who now live just west of Queensland in central Australia. She is the goddess who grows both old and young as the year changes (like Changing Woman of the Navajo; see story). Every day she reenters the womb of life under the sand where all the ancient spirits live. (See other sun goddess stories: Amaterasu, Mother Sun, Shapash, Saule.) I borrowed the seed of Merlin Stone's tale in *Ancient Mirrors of Womanhood* to write Sun Woman's story, which honors the twelve-step program admonition to live "one day at a time." I invoke Sun Woman with that slogan and have also carried a bit of red cloth and a wood chip to remind me of her.

The Tasks for Each Day

eep down under the sands of the desert live all the spirits who have died or have not yet been born. All day long the spirit people sew a huge red dress, needles flashing in and out, working seams and hems so the dress will fit just right.

The dress is for Sun Woman. Every night Sun Woman returns to the spirit people under the sand and slips into the new dress they've prepared for her. Then, just before every dawn, the spirit people give Sun Woman a huge log, which they light for her journey up to the earth people.

Each night, the spirit people make just one dress and ready just one log for one torch. That one dress and torch are what Sun Woman takes for her trip across the sky every day.

It wasn't always like that, though. About a thousand years after time began, the spirit people began to complain. "We're tired of making a dress every night," they said. "Sun Woman won't mind if we make a hundred dresses and pile them up. That way we can take a vacation. We can stack up lots of logs for her torches, too."

It was summertime then, and Sun Woman was old. It took her a long time to cross the sky. That evening when she hobbled under the desert sands for the night, the spirit people gathered about her.

"Sun Woman, Sun Woman," they said. "We're tired of sewing every night. It's the same thing over and over again. Sun Woman, we want to work very hard for a while and pile up a lot of dresses and logs, and then we want to rest."

Sun Woman surprised the spirit people with her answer. "I'm tired too," she said. She let out a big sigh and sat down heavily. "I'm exhausted. Forget about making dresses and getting torches," she said. "I'm too tired to go up to the earth people for a while."

The spirit people looked at one another. "But, Sun Woman," they said, "if you don't go up there, there won't be any daytime."

Sun Woman shrugged. "If you can take a vacation, so can I," she said.

The spirit people looked at one another again. Then an old woman spirit spoke out. "I know about being tired, Sun Woman," she said. "I lived a very long time among the earth people. My life there was very hard. But every morning, Sun Woman, you came again out of the ground, and there before me was a new day. I needed you, Sun Woman. I needed your light so I could keep on."

Then an old man spirit began to speak. "I lost my wife and children when I was a young man," he said. " 'I cannot face my life without my family,' I said. 'I want to die.' But my friend came and held my hands. 'Don't face all the days of your life,' my friend said. 'Just face today. See. Here comes Sun Woman. Just stay this one day, until she leaves us tonight.' " The old man spirit stopped for a moment. Then he said, "That's what I did. I stayed just for one day. And I kept doing that. Just staying for one day each day. That's how I lived for a long time—one day at a time."

"Sun Woman," said a baby spirit. "If you don't make your journey every day, I don't want to be born."

The spirit people nodded and talked aloud together. "The earth people need Sun Woman. And Sun Woman needs us," they said.

Sun Woman soaked her feet as she listened.

That night the spirit people and Sun Woman agreed that no one would take a vacation. The spirit people would ready one dress and one log for each of Sun Woman's journeys. And Sun Woman would travel up to the earth people and cross their sky every day.

That's how it's been ever since. Sometimes Sun Woman is young, and then she hurries across the sky. Sometimes she is old, and then she walks very slowly. But always she comes, and always she returns to the land under the desert sands where the spirit people busy themselves with the one red dress and one burning log for each day.

Cerridwen, Queen of Wisdom

(SAIR-i-dwen)

Wales

Introduction

The Celtic people, called the Gauls by the Romans, once populated lands extending from the mouth of the Danube in Romania to the western coast of France. Called Galatians in ancient Poland and Spain, they were also the Galatians of ancient Turkey, to whom the Christian Paul wrote the missionary letter of the New Testament. In a saga that mirrors that of earth-revering peoples today, this many-tribed and -languaged group fled continually from Roman, Teuton, Angle, Saxon, and Jute invaders until they finally came to occupy only the outskirts of their once tremendous territory: today's Ireland, Scotland, Wales, Cornwall, and Brittany. Settled in this island world, they received the gift of writing from the goddess Bridget (see story) and began to record their oral traditions.

In the context of legends that remember women as governmental, martial, political, and oracular leaders, Celtic storytellers told of Cerridwen, who personified the religious mystery central to the

Celts: reincarnation within the womb of the goddess. Cerridwen's name means "cauldron of wisdom," the vessel of disintegration and rebirth, a concept that celebrates the cyclical rather than linear nature of time. The cauldron, paralleling the Christian cross or sword, is a pivotal symbol for goddess worshippers the world over. It is called by Hindus the pot of blood in Kali's hand (see story of Kali), and by Egyptians the underworld womb or lake of fire. (The latter concept was borrowed by Christian storytellers for their underworld hell.) The cauldron is the precursor to the Christian holy grail or the mythological chalice of Christ's last supper. The Celts said that the endlessly boiling cauldron was stirred by nine sisters (see Bridget's story). The Nine Sisters represent the holy trinity of maiden, mother, and crone, each able to manifest all three of her selves. They are related to both the nine muses of Greek mythology and Chinese stories in which the great goddess was represented by nine tripod mixing vessels.

The cauldron's magic, like the goddess's own, is that of endlessly shifting shapes. Shamanic initiations in many cultures include halluci-natory experiences of psychic dismemberment, boiling, and rebirth in the pot of the world (see stories of Inanna and Ereshkigal, Sedna, Isis, and Mayahuel). The "year and a day" required for initiation in Celtic mythology (a time span often encoded in today's fairy tales) refers to the thirteen twenty-eight-day lunar months of a year with one more day to make 365 days.

Cerridwen, as the dark aspect of the triple goddess, also took the form for the Celts of the sacred sow. In this form, she symbolized earth, giver of life and death. In an excellent example of cross-cul-tural symbolism, Cerridwen shared her pig shape with the goddesses Freya, Demeter, and Astarte (see stories). Ancient peoples in Spain and Malta, as well, worshipped the goddess as mother pig in sacred rites.

I invented Cerridwen's story, basing it on the one told by Merlin Stone in *Ancient Mirrors of Womanhood*. That story, in turn, was put together from the sixteenth century work of the Welsh Elis Grufydd, who collected and recorded verbal accounts of ancient beliefs.

Cerridwen, for me, is a mixture of Inanna and Ereshkigal; her transformative powers parallel those of Isis. But I call on Cerridwen when the concern at hand is socially shocking or horrifying. To invoke her, I make a fire of herbs or rubbing alcohol in a small, lidded, iron cauldron.

The Cauldron of Magic
and Regeneration

t the beginning, Cerridwen, queen of wisdom, took the form of a huge bird and swallowed a piece of the sky. When, afterward, she felt life stir within her, she flew to the mountain where the nine sisters live. There, with the sisters moaning and shuddering about her, she took the form of woman among them and began to swell with life. Truly then she was wondrous to behold: eyes blue as the day sky, skin black as the night sky, and hair the color of the sun.

And so it was that Cerridwen, queen of wisdom, made her home on the mountain of the nine sisters—three forever young, three forever in the middle of life, and three forever old.

Cerridwen's child was born under the light of a star. When her own moaning finally ceased and she held the boy bloody in her arms, she washed him clean with her tears and sang him a thousand little songs. Like his mother, the boy's skin was black as night and his hair as hard to look at as the sun. But instead of day-sky eyes, the boy's eyes were brown like the wings of his mother when she'd conceived him.

Cerridwen named the boy Morfran. She saw how curious he was, how his tiny fingers explored every stone and flower. She knew that someday she wanted him to drink from the cauldron of the deep, from which all things come and to which all things return. With the nine sisters, she resolved to ready him for that day when he would drink from the source of her wisdom.

The goddesses respected the boy, and so Morfran grew to respect himself, the mountain, Cerridwen, and the nine sisters. He played with every herb and root that grew on the mountain. He learned the movements of the sun, the moon, and the stars. He sipped up the changes of the rains, the rivers, and the animals.

The day came when Cerridwen knew that her plan for her son could be realized. She saw that he honored himself, his mountain, and his family. She marked just thirteen moons from Morfran's thirteenth year. Then would be the time for him to drink from the cauldron of the deep.

Onto the fire tended by the nine sisters, Cerridwen and Morfran swung a huge black pot. Into it they dropped herbs and roots, each picked at the proper moment in the movement of the planets. From the faraway sea, they added the foam of inspiration and prophecy and, from the clouds in the sky, they stirred in the ability to change shape.

Cerridwen chanted this chant as they readied the cauldron:

> *That you know what you know*
> *And see what you see:*
> *This is the brew I brew for thee.*
> *In my cauldron deep I brew this brew,*
> *that wisdom walk far when it walk with you.*

A year and a day they would stir. Then Morfran would taste its first three magic drops.

One day, as Morfran sat at the side of the cauldron, he was startled to see someone very like himself appear on the other side of the billowing smoke. This stranger was clearly a boy, but he was larger than Morfran, with skin so pale that purplish blue marks showed on it. The boy drew back when he saw Morfran and covered his eyes against the brightness of Morfran's hair.

"Who are you?" asked Morfran.

"Gwion," said the boy.

"Where do you come from?" asked Morfran.

"The valley."

"Who is your mother?" asked Morfran.

The boy said nothing. Then he tried to look at Morfran. "I can't look at your head," he said. "It's too bright."

"It's my mother's hair," said Morfran. Then he scooped up some ash from the fire and rubbed it in his hair. "Look now."

The boy looked. The brilliance dulled, he could keep his eyes on Morfran.

The boy looked frightened and hungry. When Morfran handed him a bowl of stew, the boy shoveled the food to his mouth as fast as he could.

"Who is your mother?" asked Morfran again when Gwion had finished.

"My mother is the richest, nicest queen in the world, and my father is the strongest, most wonderful king," he said loudly.

That evening Cerridwen tied a cloth around her head so Gwion could look at her. Cerridwen, the nine sisters, and Morfran shared food and made a bed for Gwion. They listened as he boasted about how powerful and good his parents were. When Cerridwen asked him why he'd left his parents, Gwion said he was tired and went to bed.

Cerridwen and Morfran sat together in the dark. "Mother," said Morfran. "Gwion isn't well and he's lying about his parents."

Cerridwen pulled Morfran close. "What a magician you're going to be," she said, "when you are so wise already."

The next day Cerridwen asked Gwion how he'd gotten the bruises on his arms and legs. Gwion began to cry. Cerridwen opened her arms to him, and with the nine sisters circling them, Gwion admitted that his parents were neither king nor queen. They beat him, he said, and sometimes he wasn't sure they even knew his name.

"You are welcome here on the mountain," said Cerridwen.

So Gwion stayed. He found that he'd come to the mountain of Cerridwen, queen of wisdom, and that her son Morfran was stirring the cauldron of the deep, from which all things come and to which all things return. In less than a year and a day now Morfran would drink the first three drops of the cauldron's brew and would walk in wisdom and magic.

Gwion had never felt so safe and free. Sometimes he pretended that Cerridwen was his mother and Morfran his brother. But other times, the pain and loneliness of his time in the valley rose up inside him. Gwion was sure his parents had been mean to him because he was bad.

In his secret heart, Gwion began to hate Morfran. Even though he helped Morfran stir the brew, played games with him at the side of the fire, and told stories with him at night, envy ate at his heart. He told himself that Morfran was ugly and weak.

As the year and a day drew to a close, Gwion began to ask himself why it should be Morfran who got to drink the first three drops from the cauldron of the deep. "He has everything," said Gwion to himself. "Why should he, and not I, get those drops?"

As the brew neared its time, it grew thicker and harder to stir. On the night before Morfran was to turn thirteen, Cerridwen stirred the cauldron the whole night long. In the morning, Morfran took her place. "Soon, son," said Cerridwen. She smiled at him, blue eyes shining with pride.

Gwion wished he had a mother who would look at him like that. Today, he even liked Morfran. "But it's not fair," he told himself.

Then he tensed. Gwion saw that Cerridwen had gone away to rest. Morfran was looking into the fire, his face calm, eyes glowing.

Then Gwion saw that Cerridwen had fallen asleep.

"It's ready, Gwion," said Morfran softly.

Something burst inside of Gwion. He ran at Morfran and shoved him as hard as he could. Then three times he dipped the tip of his own finger into the huge pot. When he'd tasted the third drop, the cauldron split in two with a roar. The liquid inside smothered the fire underneath and poured out all over the ground.

Morfran shouted. Cerridwen awoke from her nap. With a cry of rage, she tore the cloth from her fiery hair and lunged after Gwion.

Terrified, Gwion used the magic now inside him to turn himself into a rabbit. He leapt away, and Cerridwen turned herself into a greyhound and bounded after him. Just as she was about to catch him, Gwion changed to a fish and plunged into a river. Cerridwen's body took the shape of an otter and dove at the tail of the fish. Nearly out of strength, Gwion turned himself into a tiny bird and shuddered to see that Cerridwen was now a giant hawk gaining on him with every push of her wings.

Exhausted now, Gwion spied, in the valley from which he'd come, a pile of wheat. There he plummeted and turned himself into a tiny piece of grain.

Cerridwen turned herself then into a black-crested hen in that yard with the pile of wheat, and she pecked and pecked until she'd eaten the boy whole.

Then, for a second time, Cerridwen the bird felt life growing in her. But this time, when she went to the mountain with the nine sisters, her son was there, and Cerridwen had rage in her heart. This child inside her had taken from her son what was rightfully his. She swore she would never let this boy inside her live. She waited out the birth, knowing she would kill him when he was born.

But when the baby came and she held it bloody in her arms, she could not bear to kill it.

No one knows what happened to Gwion. Some say Gwion got his wish and that Cerridwen herself raised him as her second son. Others say that he was raised in the valley from where he'd come, but this time by parents who respected him. Those people say he became a great poet and magician who could change his shape at will and tell the future.

The nine sisters, it is said, pieced together the cauldron of the deep. On the mountain they stir it still, keepers of the place from which all things come and to which all things return.

And Morfran? No one knows either what became of him. But many say he walks the earth still, hair gray from the ashes he dusted there so long ago. He is not a poet or a magician, people say, but a wise man who knows what he knows and sees what he sees.

Maya, Masked Woman
of the Primordial Void

(MY-yuh)

India

Introduction

The goddess Maya of India is the relentless process of life itself. The spell of Maya is blind life energy continuously manifesting itself: originating, growing, decaying, and vanishing, forever veiling from her creatures the true nature of her void. Maya is the neutral screen on which the endless characters and plots of our souls' moving pictures project and complete their dramas. She is the inward dream of the senses and the cosmic mystery, mixing the desires of human hearts and supernatural tensions in a paradox of wisdom and enchantment. In Maya, there is nothing static, nothing abiding. Demonic and beneficent, she is the name of our illusion and delusion: her face both beguiles and opens the way to transcendent enlightenment.

Hindu mythology dresses the mystery of the world in fantastic personifications. Maya, like the Shakti, Kali (a form of the Shakti), and Devi (see stories), are all manifestations of the primordial feminine in whose embrace the great masculine energies of Brahma, Vishnu, and Shiva come to throbbing, proliferating, and perishing life. Although

171

most renditions of Hindu mythologies suffer from the pervasiveness of patriarchal bias, today's actual worship of the great feminine in India is explicit and inspiringly current.

Maya's name is shared by goddesses of mystery and illusion in many parts of the world. Central Americans called her Mayahuel (see story); the Greeks called her Maia; the Irish, Maga; and the Scandinavians, Maj.

Maya's story has something of the flavor of a Zen koan and is a retelling of the traditional one recounted by Heinrich Zimmer in *Myths and Symbols in Indian Art and Culture*. The movie *Cinema Paradiso* is a brilliant evocation of Maya. I think of her when I play with a kaleidoscope; this goddess helps me come to terms with both my need to make sense of the workings of the universe and my sometimes overwhelming sense of its meaninglessness.

The Goddess
Behind the God

t happened that the saint Narada had practiced so long and thoroughly the renuncia-
tion of the things of the earthly plane that
the god Vishnu himself went walking with
him. The two talked deeply about many
things. But the god Vishnu only smiled enigmatically when Narada
asked that he be allowed to know the great Vishnu's Maya.

Narada insisted, however, and said, "Great Vishnu, I know that you
yourself are only a manifestation of your Maya. If I am to truly know
you, my lord, I must know the goddess from whom you come."

Vishnu curved his beautiful lips and told Narada that he recom-
mended the contentment that came with their own friendship. He said
that knowledge of the Maya was too much of an undertaking, even for
such a one as the saint Narada.

Narada was silent awhile as he and Vishnu strolled in the sheltered
hermit's grove. Though they talked of other things, it happened that

Narada persisted in his plea to know the real power of the god, and Vishnu finally shrugged and relented.

He took Narada to a place on the desert where the heat shimmered in the sands and the white ball of the sun seemed to scorch the very blood. Narada's thirst grew, but he rested in the knowledge that soon he would know the Maya of the world.

"Narada, I am thirsty," said Vishnu finally. He pointed in the direction of a tiny hamlet of houses moving in and out of their vision like waves in the light. "Pray go to the first house and bring me a glass of water."

Narada bowed and made his way across the burning hills to the first house. He knocked.

When the door opened, a young woman greeted Narada and bade him enter, gazing at him all the while with eyes that filled Narada suddenly and completely with mysterious feeling. And it happened that the feeling so overtook Narada that he simply forgot why he had come.

His eyes with the woman's seemed to lock, and he continued to return to their depths as he drank from her dipper of water. How very like his lord's they were! How kind and fathomless at once!

Soon Narada met her family in the next room. Her father and mother sat at a feast table, along with three brothers, all of whom had wives and beautiful children. Like the woman herself, none of the family commented on his arrival but seemed to accept him as if they'd known he was coming.

The foods of the evening were sumptuous, and Narada felt himself held in a sweetness of pleasure. It was a sensation—what with the delicacies and the eyes and conversation of this woman—like none he had ever known before.

It came to pass that there flowered between Narada and the woman a friendship that brought both peace and joy and an enthusiasm for the future. Before long, the two had wed, and all the village rejoiced.

Eleven years went by. Narada joined with the family of his wife in the seasonal tasks of farm and home. He and the woman had three children. Narada felt richness and gratitude overflow in his heart.

In the twelfth year, the rains came with a fury rarely seen. Straw huts and cattle were carried away on their torrent, and people fled. One howling night, the waters began to flood the house. Narada woke his wife and their children, and, clinging to each other, the family made its way into the dark. Narada carried the smallest child and held tight to the hand of the next, who in turn clutched her brother's hand. The mother clung to the hand of the eldest. The current tore at their legs, and the parents could barely manage their burdens.

Narada made himself heard over the gale that they must find the top of the hill.

Suddenly, at the moment lightning cracked the sky, a mountain of water ripped Narada's baby from his arms. With a cry, he lunged after the child and lost the girl's hand. Another stroke of lightning revealed the avalanche of water that struck Narada's wife and children. Helpless, their screams piercing his heart, Narada saw his family sucked under the deep.

The next thing Narada knew, he was atop the hill of the village, able only to weep.

Narada then felt a hand on his shoulder. He looked to find the god Vishnu beside him, shaking his head gently. "You come at last," said the god. "I have been waiting for you almost half an hour. Do you now understand the secret of my Maya?"

Mother Sun

Cherokee People

Introduction

I gaehindvo, the Cherokee Mother Sun, with her sisters Elihino, Mother Earth, and Sehu, Corn Woman, are the very tenor of life itself. The three sisters are undoubtedly of ancient origin for the Cherokee, whose name comes from the word *chiluik-ki,* meaning cave dwellers. By the early nineteenth century, however, the Cherokee Nation lived a life extraordinarily similar to that of their European-immigrant neighbors. Unlike many other native tribes, the Cherokee were not nomadic. In fact, their settlements could hardly be distinguished from other farm towns in the state of Georgia. Some Cherokee owned huge cotton plantations and black slaves. They published their own newspaper. Their government and court systems were nearly identical with those of the United States. They had even fought with the U.S. cavalry against their Creek Indian neighbors. Nonetheless, when gold was discovered on Cherokee territory, Congress gave permission in 1838 for "Indian removal." Over a six-month period, seven thousand U.S. soldiers drove fourteen thousand Cherokee west from Georgia to

Oklahoma, over what was later called the Trail of Tears. Drought, extreme cold, measles, and whooping cough struck the marchers. One of every four Cherokee died.

The tale of Mother Sun and her daughter was collected in the 1890s. (See Erdoes' and Ortiz's *American Indian Myths and Legends*.) The story-teller was likely alive, probably an adult at the time of the Trail of Tears. His wry spoof of the great mother's cantankerous quirks gives way to a myth replete with forbidden box, the how-and-why tale of a red bird, a world flood, sorrow reminiscent of the Greek Demeter's (see story), and a spirit dance recalling the Japanese Amaterasu Omikami's (see story). I invoke Mother Sun when I want to find the hidden good thing in a harsh authority figure.

The Dance of
the Grandchildren

other Sun's face was red. Pacing back and forth, she gesticulated as she spoke. Moon sat listening, a little slumped, his pale lips pressed together. He looked down sadly at Earth tilting below them. Mother Sun and Moon had had this conversation before.

"Oh, stop mooning," fumed Mother Sun.

"I feel sorry for them," said Moon.

"Well, you can afford to. They look at you like they love you—all soft and smiling. I'm sick of it."

"Mother Sun," said Moon. "They seem ugly to you because you don't realize how hard it is to look at you when you're like this."

"Like what? I'm just being myself, and they squinch up their faces in ugly pouts every time they look up here."

"They're your grandchildren," said Moon. "If they could hear you talk like this, they'd be even more upset."

"Well, I'm tired of your sniveling and I've had it with them. Maybe they can't hear me, but they're going to feel me," she said grimly.

Moon sighed. "You're a vindictive old woman," he said and faded away.

Mother Sun stalked over to her daughter's house for her usual noontime lunch.

"Mother," said Sun Daughter. "What are you doing?"

Mother Sun was standing just outside the house, arms raised high, sending down her most ferocious heat to the people below. "I'm trying to kill them," she puffed. "They're ugly and they like Moon better than me, and I'm going to punish them."

Sun Daughter watched for a while, then shook her head. "I don't know why you can't relax. Why do you insist that they act just as you want them to?"

Mother Sun paid no attention. She continued to pour out her heat.

Sun Daughter's red dress fluttered. "Come inside, Mother," she said finally. "I've got your favorite yellow squash soup."

Mother Sun, who was tired anyway, allowed herself to be led inside. But seated at the table, she continued to punctuate her rapid chewing with bitter remarks about Moon and the grandchildren.

Meanwhile, the people below were falling ill by the hundreds.

Afraid and sorrowful, they sent a group of leaders to the Little People who live under the world. The opening to the underworld was small, but once inside, so blessedly cool that the heat from the fires of the Little People even felt comforting.

"Mother Sun is trying to kill you," the Little People explained. "You must find a way to kill her instead. We will help."

In huge black cauldrons, the Little People stirred up the medicine to form four poisonous snakes.

"Send Spreading Adder and Copperhead first," they instructed. "If those two can't kill her, send the others."

Spreading Adder and Copperhead slithered to the top of the sky. Nervously, they coiled beside Sun Daughter's door. Spreading Adder flicked his tongue while Copperhead practiced his most frightening posture. But when Mother Sun strode into view, having made her journey from the other side of the sky vault, Spreading Adder cowered in her blinding light. All he could do was to spit yellow slime.

Mother Sun saw only Copperhead. "You nasty old thing," she said, and stepped over him.

Ashamed, Spreading Adder and Copperhead slunk away.

Then, during the night, Rattlesnake and Water Monster sneaked up to Sun Daughter's house. Water Monster's tail covered Moon and the stars with dark clouds. Everyone was sure Water Monster, with his terrible eyes and horns, would assassinate Mother Sun quickly and bring this plague of heat to an end.

The two reptiles lurked outside Sun Daughter's door. Rattlesnake twitched at every sound, so eager was he to be helpful.

"Would you calm down?" said Water Monster irritably. "She doesn't get here till noon."

But Rattlesnake's jumpiness got the better of him. Just before noon, when Sun Daughter opened her door to look for her mother, Rattlesnake struck and killed her.

"Fool!" shouted Water Monster. "You got the wrong one!" In a fury, he churned back to the people below. There he complained and threatened so venomously that the people had to send him to the end of the world, where he remains to this day.

Mother Sun found her daughter's body, still warm in the doorway. Her jealousy of Moon and her plans for punishing the earth broke to pieces inside her. She gathered her child in her arms. Sun Daughter's ghost peeled away from her form and trembled over the wailing mother. Then Sun Daughter's spirit flitted away to Ghost Country in the darkening land in the west.

Mother Sun shut herself inside her daughter's house and refused to come out. The people were no longer dying of heat, but now they lived in total darkness.

Once more the grandchildren asked the Little People for help.

"Send seven men with seven sticks and a good strong box to Ghost Country," instructed the Little People. "Use the sticks to capture Sun

Daughter in the box—and fetch her home. When Mother Sun has her child again, she will shine for you. But whatever you do, whatever she says, don't open that box till she's safe with her mother."

For seven days the seven men with seven sticks and a good strong box traveled to Ghost Country. Whirling in the circles of spirits dancing there, the seven men found Sun Daughter in her smoky red dress. Each time she passed, one of the men touched her with his stick. At the seventh touch, Sun Daughter rose up out of the Ghost Dance and the men folded her into the box. The dance of the Ghost People quickened. ·

Carrying the precious box, the seven men began the journey east. But before long, Sun Daughter's voice wheedled out of the box. "Please let me out!" The men looked at one another, but did not answer.

"I'm so hungry!" Sun Daughter said pitifully. "I can't breathe in here!" she moaned. "I'm dying!"

The men felt afraid. Suppose she did die and they were not able to bring her alive to her mother? The people might send them, as they had Water Monster, to the end of the world. The men shrugged helplessly. They opened the box a tiny crack.

With a fluttering, something flew past them. A bright redbird lit on a nearby bush. Frightened, the men opened the box all the way. Sun Daughter was gone! But in her new form of redbird, she began to warble a song. In great dismay, the men tried to catch her. But Sun Daughter, forever redbird now, took wing. If only the men had kept the box closed, we would always have been able to bring back the people we love from the Ghost Country. But alas, it isn't so! The men shut the lid on the empty box and forced themselves to return to the settlements.

Mother Sun screamed when she opened the box. When she'd heard of the seven men's journey, she had clung to the hope that she might be able to see her child again. Now she understood that her daughter would never come back. She wept tears that flooded the entire world.

In hopes of saving themselves from the drowning darkness, the people held council. They sent up a group of children to drum and dance for Mother Sun. Clinging to one another's hands, the young-sters danced the most winning dance they could. Mother Sun, how-ever, seemed to pay no attention. All was dark, wet, and freezing cold.

Then, without warning, the drummers changed their beat. The dancers dropped hands, and each began a separate leaping and twirling, faster and faster. The quickened rhythm was so exciting that Mother Sun stopped crying and could not help herself from peeking. When they saw her face, the dancers rippled into a rainbow of joy.

Mother Sun's eyes filled again with tears. But this time she did not spill them. She gazed at her dancing and singing grandchildren. How alive they were! And not ugly at all. Mother Sun smiled tremulously and opened the door. Stepping outside, she, very gently, raised her arms.

VI

Goddess as Archetype

S tories of the primordial feminine re-synthesize the power of femaleness hidden and maligned by a culture that polarizes both actual and ideological gender, and still so persistently elevates what is associated with the masculine at the expense of what is imagined to be the feminine. Despite current social equalities between the genders that would have been unthinkable even a remarkably short time ago, we have enormous trouble integrating at the level of the collective unconscious the elixir of the feminine in all of us. This is almost certainly due to the culture's persistent erasure and diabolization of the divine feminine. The implications of this are stifling for all who are identified with Other—women, children, people of color, people with other than heterosexualities, plants, animals, indeed the earth herself.

Goddess stories begin to glue together the archetype of the great feminine that has been shattered by the culture's stereotypes and habits of repression. Even if we choose not to worship her, we find in goddess stories images of our true inner and outer selves. Goddess changes our posture: no longer do great and feminine seem contradictions in terms. Like children with role models, our eyes melt before these ways we can copy, and we find ourselves growing—feet sure, stomachs round, voices bold and free. Our relationships with body, earth, self, and each other are come new.

Mbaba Mwana Waresa,
Great Rain Mother of All

(mah-BAH-bah mah-WAH-nah wah-REH-sah)
Zulu

Introduction

The oldest human remains and the earliest human tools ever made
have both been found on the continent of Africa, in today's Kenya
and Tanzania. From this vast land, which stretches five thousand miles
north to south and likewise east to west, come the human ancestors of
early European culture and the divine ancestress herself. In those beginning times, from 30,000 to 15,000 B.C.E., when politics and religion
were one, nearly identical paintings that froze the sacred life spirits on
the womb walls of caves have been found in ancient France and Spain,
South Africa, Zimbabwe, Morocco, Libya, and around the Sahara
Desert. As from the center of a great web, the peoples of Africa must
have migrated over the millennia to the slender ends of their world. The
bone characteristics of the skeletal remains of ancient Europeans show
unmistakably their black African heritage.

Out of Africa, the cradle of a thousand human cultures, rises the goddess by as many names. The Zulu people of Natal, South Africa, understood her, like so many people the world over, as personifying the water

of life. Other peoples worship her in the river, the lake, and the ocean (see story of Yemaya and Iamanja). The Zulu call her mother of rain, Mbaba Mwana Waresa.

Since the Zulu are renowned for their beautiful and complicated dances for all sacred occasions, her traditional story in this collection, adapted from the one told in *Ancient Mirrors of Womanhood,* may well enact a reverential dance for rain. The October sky actually sprinkled a couple of years ago during a Berkeley evening of telling her story and chanting her name. I dream of the day we take to the streets, *en masse,* with pots and pans in honor of her water. Mbaba's story also pricks me with hope about our far-reaching abilities to take back the idea of beauty from the mongers of self-hatred.

The Choice of the
Wise Husband

ver the green, brown, and blue earth lives the sky mama. Ma-baba. In the lightning and thunder hear her voice and her drums. Ma-wana. The glistening, the slicking, the wa-wet drops slanting, sleeking down are her arms and her legs, her hands and her feet. Wa-resa.

> Ma-baba Ma-wana Wa-resa.
> In the rainbow is her smile.
> Mbaba Mwana Waresa.
> Mbaba Mwana Waresa.

It is Mbaba Mwana Waresa who pours down her sacred waters to her thirsty people, plants, animals, lakes, and rivers.

Mbaba Mwana Waresa cleans, cools, quenches, fills, soaks, pounds, drizzles, and streams. Mbaba Mwana Waresa, rain mother of all, is the one without whom there is no life.

In her absence we long for her, dance for her. Mbaba! we cry. Mwana! Waresa! Gone too long, we die, Mbaba. Come to us!

In her presence we put away our fans. We are thankful. We collect her sacred waters in our pots. We shiver and dream of fire. Mbaba! Mwana! Waresa! Your noise is mighty. The night is long. We want a fire and a story.

The fire is built. Here is the story.

Once upon a time Mbaba Mwana Waresa wished for a husband. When none of the gods in heaven pleased her, she went to earth to look for the wisest, most handsome man she could find. When the young man she had chosen heard tell he was to marry Mbaba Mwana Waresa, he went away by himself for a long while to think and prepare himself.

Mbaba Mwana Waresa returned to heaven to ready herself for the wedding. But to the astonishment of all in heaven, Mbaba Mwana Waresa did nothing to decorate herself. Instead she asked her friend to dress as the Zulu bride. Wondering at Mbaba's request, her friend had the finest clothes wrapped about her body and her hair braided into a hundred delicate plaits with beautiful beads laced at each end. Gold and silver bracelets were coiled at her wrists and ankles, and sacred dyes were painted on her cheeks and forehead. Great hoops were hung in her ears, and shining stones threaded on thin copper wires beneath her arms jingled softly as she moved. The womb shell of life was hung on her forehead.

When Mbaba Mwana Waresa saw that her friend was ready, she did an even stranger thing. She removed all her own precious beads and her rainbow-colored robes. With a sharp stone she cut all the tiny beautiful curls from her head. She smeared her smooth black skin with pale gray ashes and wrapped herself in the torn skin of a zebra.

Then Mbaba Mwana Waresa declared that the heavenly pair was ready to make the journey to the village where the young groom awaited her.

The young man knew the wedding day had come when the sky above him darkened and lightning cracked across the clouds. He heard the beat of her drums in the thunder that followed. The young man held his shoulders very straight as he went to stand in the rain of his good fortune.

The women from the village chosen as wedding attendants gathered with him, and when the goddess and her friend arrived, everyone bowed low in reverence. Then all watched to see if the young man would know which of the two from heaven was to be his wife.

The young man did not hesitate. He extended his hands to Mbaba Mwana Waresa, knowing her even in the torn skin of a zebra, body gray with ashes, and the hair of her lovely head shaved away.

"Welcome, Mbaba Mwana Waresa," said the young man. "You need no precious beads, nor fine clothes, nor silver and gold jewelry to show me who you are. For I see in your eyes the richness of the earth, the bounty of the harvest, and the power of your thunder and lightning. How honored I am to be your husband."

Mbaba Mwana Waresa smiled. She had chosen well, for this young man was wise enough to see the truth. The friend of Mbaba Mwana Waresa and all the attendants began to clap and sing. The wedding ceremony was held, and then Mbaba Mwana Waresa took her husband back to heaven, where he lives with her to this very day. Mbaba Mwana Waresa.

Juno, Mother of the World

(JEW -no)

Rome

Introduction

L ike Freya of northern Europe and Isis of Egypt (see stories), Juno, the supreme Roman goddess, was far too powerful to be fully subordinated by the patriarchy. Instead, her glory persisted, and she took dozens of forms for her worshippers. As Juno Fortuna, she was Mistress of Fate; as Regina, she reigned Queen of Heaven. As Juno Moneta, she gave us the word money and was the great adviser and admonisher. Juno Februa was goddess of erotic love; Juno Populonia was mother of the people. As Juno Lucina, queen of celestial light, she is related to her Greek counterpart, Hera, from whose breasts stream the Milky Way. Scandinavian countries preserve Lucina in maiden form at the winter solstice by having a girl with a crown of candles and white gown reenact her bringing of the light.

The name *juno* is cognate to the Etruscan *uni,* root of the word *universe,* and to *yoni,* the name for the sacred vulva and womb of all life. Her lily, or lotus, the universal symbol for the yoni, enabled this three-in-one divine mother to conceive the god Mars without the aid of her consort Jupiter. Thus, she was called the Blessed Virgin, a title borrowed by Christian storytellers for their Mary.

Every woman embodied a portion of the great Juno in her *juno* or soul, corresponding to the *genius* in every man. Patriarchal vocabularies dropped the word *juno*, retaining and elevating the word *genius* and, unfortunately, depriving women of their souls, lexicographically speaking. Her sacred month was June, in which she oversaw marriages and family matters. June is believed to this day to be the luckiest month for weddings.

Over the centuries of the Common Era, the Church solidified the new story of Mary, the virgin girl impregnated with the light of the world. Just beneath this story, of course, was the old story of the great mother of the world who self-impregnates or mates with her own son-sun, the year, to give birth once again to the light's cycle of life and death.

This ancient understanding does not condone human incest. Both goddess and god, though strongly personified, are about the archetypal generative powers that work in the world and in humans but which are deeper and more mysterious than we can easily comprehend without the aid of personification. These archetypes work without and within, marrying the worlds and our own parts together again and again. (See stories of Mary, Isis, Nu Kua, and Mayahuel.)

In the Temple
of Her Lap

hen the rain black sky kisses the ridge of
the mountain and the water pours from the
throats of the clouds; when the undersides
of tree leaves lick up the wind; when the
octopus wraps, beak to beak, jet to jet, her
beloved; when whales moan and the sea horse pockets his young; when
irises spread purple to cream; when grasses fan and she-wolves dream;
when lace green shrubs settle haunches on earth; when the lather of the
sea caresses the shore; when buck mounts doe and the teats of the bear
distend; when bees plunge soft into the necks of their flowers: now is the
time when every mating thing groans and struts, and climbs onto the
secret raft of together. Now is the time when gold nestles in its rock, the
time in the sound and the silence when the goddess Juno, Mars for one
eye and Venus for the other, drops the coins from her purses, and gathers
to her lap her sun king, the bayingly beautiful year, the child of her heart
and thighs. Ecstatic, majestic, they make for us again another sun.

Here is the Light Queen holding her precious son: opening, letting, giving. Here is the breaking down and the building up, the weeping and the laughing, the gathering. Now the casting away. Opening, letting, giving, gone.

Now the boy-man-sun-son grows bent and soft, hairless and gentle. Now out of the west comes the boat with the blinding sails. Now the Juno and her king are clinging, mourning.

Now the seed sleeps under the ground. Now the pumpkins orange and the persimmon trees drop their leaves and swell their fruits; now the roses and the hawthornes are twilit gray.

Now the great circles separate. After the glorious one, there are two. Now is the good-bye. Now is the waving and waving to the son-sun on his boat with the fire bright sails. Now is the slipping away, the shore of death.

The night doves purl and the cave is sealing itself. Juno Lucina is closing the temple of her lap. Now is the waiting. Now is the cave of life.

Container of containers is the great Juno. Her hands hold the rings of ice and fire. Her fingers are the choices, her eyes the twirling knowings of the worlds.

Now when the farm animals kneel and the dogs bow to the east, here is the ending and the beginning. For Juno so loved the world that she gave herself to the son she most desired. For Juno so loved that she gave away the uppermost desire of her heart, that she might flow with the circle of the everlasting. For Juno so loved that she opened herself to ending that she might hold death, that the son might perish, that the sun of the east might spring to light from that perishing.

Demeter and Persephone, Keepers of the Mystery of the Planted Seed

(DEM-uh-ter and per-SEF-uh-nee)
Greece

Introduction

The goddess Demeter was once the mother of the great triangle of life, the mystery of the universe, complete in all her parts: creator, preserver, destroyer. *Meter* means "mother," and *de* is the word for delta, the triangle-shaped letter of the Greek alphabet. Her name was thus a visual pun: it suggested both the sacred vulva and the great three-in-one mother. The goddess Persephone, who later came to be seen as maiden, daughter of Demeter, and simultaneously queen of the underworld, was once simply another way of talking about the goddess Demeter in her virgin and crone aspects. (See the story of Baubo for an exploration of another aspect of the crone in this story.)

Classical Greek storytellers, however, working with a masculinized pantheon of deities, regularly split the great mother into many personalities, each with her own superhuman story. The great one was thus shaved into the mothers, daughters, sisters, wives, consorts, and victims of the gods, raising to new heights the level of instruction about the workings of the relatively recently established patriarchal system.

The story of Demeter once recapitulated the mystery of the planted seed. Her journey from flower to fruit, from seed to burial, and death to rebirth was once told annually in a healing ritual called the Eleusinian mysteries, which ancient writers praise but do not detail. In the mystery ritual, the daughter of Demeter was like the seed in the fruit. As the fruit holds the seed, so every seed holds the fruited plant within herself, and so on endlessly.

Of course, separating the goddess by name and aspect can help to more deeply understand her complexity. But patriarchal bias in this case did more to the how-and-why tale of the seed and its seasons than merely splitting the goddess into mother and daughter aspects. In the story of the kidnapping and rape of Persephone by the god of the underworld, this bias not only masculinized Hades, the originally feminine deity of the deep, but postulated that rape is the maiden's introduction into her sexuality. This story may well have reflected a terribly growing reality in a culture newly given to exercising power over people, places, and things, rather than to cultivating a reverence for the power alive in every being.

My tale of Demeter and Persephone preserves the expression of the great goddess as mother and daughter. However, wisdom, growth, and the emergence of adult sexuality in this story are not predicated on the maiden's victimization, but on her choice to plumb her own depths. Grains, seeds, jewels, and rocks all symbolize these goddesses for me. We mothers and aunts can invoke Demeter and Persephone with flowers, bath, and song at the passages of our children—when they first bleed, when they first leave home.

The Beginning
of the Four Seasons

nce upon a time, a long, long time ago, there were no seasons. There were no changes in the weather or the plants. Animals played outside all the time, because the only season the earth knew was spring. Always there were hopping birds, chirping flowers, and fluffy clouds in a blue, blue sky.

That was the time when the great goddess Demeter and her daughter Persephone roamed the meadows and the hills, picking flowers, laughing, and swimming in rivers that took them whoosh! down to the next curve. There they climbed from the water, skins glistening in the sun, and ran back to throw themselves in again, rush down in the water perfect around them, and start all over again. They did everything together, Demeter and Persephone: they ate of pears, apples, and oranges. They picked bananas, persimmons, pomegranates, and grapes. They made grass and flower salads with dew for dressing and necklaces of berries and nuts. They braided strands of golden barley into each other's hair.

Demeter loved to sit on a rock and watch her daughter's brown legs flash when she ran with deer and wolf. Then she would loop her skirts and join, and the earth would bustle with the sound of feet and bees.

Demeter was so glad to have this girl. Persephone was her friend and mirror, and sometimes Demeter hugged her grown-up baby for joy.

One day Persephone wandered away for a longer time than she ever had before. When she came home to Demeter, she was quiet, and her eyes looked far away. "Where have you been, my baby?" asked Demeter, tipping Persephone's chin up a little.

Persephone moved her head down. "Out, Mother," said Persephone.

"What's wrong, little one?" asked her mother.

"Nothing," said Persephone. "And I'm not little."

Her mother fanned her hand through Persephone's curls. "Of course you're not, my baby," she said. "Of course you're not. Now come eat."

So they supped and laughed. But the next day, Persephone stayed away a long time again.

When she came back, Demeter took both her hands. "Tell me," she said. "Sit down and tell me."

"I have to go," Persephone whispered.

"Speak up, Persephone," said her mother. "You have to what?"

"I have to go," said Persephone.

"You what?" said her mother.

"I have to go away from you."

"What are you saying? What can you mean? You can't go. Persephone, we have everything here. We have the world, the whole world. What do you mean? Why? Where would you go?"

"I have to go, Mother. Down. I have to go under the earth. There are jewels there, Mommy. I have to go."

"Oh, my darling child. You can't. You can't go. It isn't safe. Tell me you won't go."

Persephone loosed her hands from her mother's. "Let's eat, Mommy," she said.

The next day, Demeter stood looking and looking for her daughter. When she finally came, Demeter grabbed her and held her. "Don't go. Oh, don't go, Persephone." The two of them rocked back and forth, holding each other in the sun.

Finally, Persephone pushed away. Tears were on both faces. "I have to go. I don't know when I'll be back, but I'll be back. Good-bye." She threw a cloak over her shoulders. As she ran, it billowed out behind her like a sail.

Demeter stood frozen for an instant. Then she let out a cry, "NO!" and leapt after her daughter. She drew just near enough to see a huge rock rumble aside, Persephone disappear, and the rock move again over the opening.

Demeter flung herself at the rock. It did not move. She moaned and steadied herself. Then she eased herself down and held her head in her hands. For a long time her shoulders shook silently. Night came. She stayed.

Neither did she move the next day. She sat still and spoke to no one. For a week she did not change her place. She did not eat. There were circles under her eyes. A sore grew on her mouth.

When she shifted her posture the next week, it was only to pull her robe more tightly about her. For the wind, always before easy and warm, had grown strong and cold.

Demeter's hair knotted in the wind. The birds and animals who had not heard her voice in so long went away. Demeter tipped her head up to the sky. "I wish only for a blanket to cover me," she cried out. And something white began to fall from the sky. It swirled and turned. Silently it began to cover the ground.

Demeter slept through the night and part of the next day.

When she awoke the sky was gray, and all around her and on her feet and arms was the white blanket called snow.

The trees scratched at the sky. No food could be found.

And still Demeter did not move.

Days and weeks went by. They turned into months.

Then one day, the sun was warm enough to begin to melt the

blanket of snow. Demeter licked her dry lips. Then she shrugged. With a great effort, she pushed herself to her feet. As soon as she did so, something came out of the ground where she had been sitting so long. A flower! A tiny white flower.

Then Demeter felt the ground beneath her move. The rock on which she'd sat uprooted itself and uncovered a flight of stairs leading down into the earth. Demeter made a sharp noise and braced herself against the rock. She peered into the opening.

Up the stairway came a girl—trudging a little, as if she were tired, but with her face turned upward. She was holding to her waist the hem of her skirt, as if there were something bumpy and heavy inside.

Demeter stood frozen. Then the sun glinted off the girl's curls.

"Persephone!"

"Mommy!" sang out the girl, and she leapt up the last steps and into her mother's arms.

When she did so, she let loose the front of her robes, and a thousand emeralds, rubies and sapphires, amethysts and diamonds spilled out on the ground. And at each place they touched, the snow melted and a host of flowers sprang up—until all the ground around those dancing goddesses was green and sparkling and the birds and animals were kicking and swooping with joy.

Now every year, since that time, we have spring only once a year. We also have summer and fall to honor the time Persephone is growing and getting ready to go to the center of the earth. And we have winter, to honor the time when Demeter's heart is breaking for missing her daughter.

Mayahuel, Endlessly Milking One

(MY-uh-you-EL)

Central America

Introduction

M other goddess Mayahuel of the Mexican agave plant is called Woman With Four Hundred Breasts. The agave plant, known as the tree of life, is spiral shaped. Its central bulb is a kind of cave dripping with a milky elixir that is fermented to make pulque, the Mexican national beverage. It is drunk in order to nourish the crops, to celebrate the harvest, and to call for longevity in this world and the next. People use the milk of the goddess plant for birth ceremonies involving the umbilical cord and baptism.

Mayahuel, mother pot of the world, is imagined as a frog with a mouth in every joint of her body; as the lady on the turquoise throne; and as mother to a suckling fish. Her story, connected to those of other cultures around the world, dates far beyond recorded Central American history. Her name and her role as goddess of pleasure, intoxication, and hallucination are both related to Maya of India (see story), goddess of the stuff of life's illusion. She was called Maia by the Greeks, Maga by the Irish, and Maj by the Scandinavians. Like the archaic Greek

Artemis, Mayahuel has many breasts and suckles a fish, the powerful symbol of transformation used also by the Christians for their own fish son, Jesus. Her consort, Ehecatl (eh-HEH-cahtle), the wind god, is related to both Quetzalcoatl and Tlaloc, whose images as the serpent and the rain suggest not an opposition to earth, but a blessed marriage of two forces, earth and sky, who need each other for the world to go on.

I regard the story of Mayahuel as a pre-Christian story of Mary and Christ, replete with the tremendously powerful archetypal themes of birth, separation, death, sacrifice, and rebirth. Indeed, in order to milk for myself an understanding of Mayahuel's story, I walked in a graveyard and told myself the Jesus story of my childhood. Reluctant at first to delve again into a saga in which Mary's part, for example, seems so bridled and meek, I was arrested instead by the Bible story's characters, whose passion, tenderness, and courage lie just beneath the veil of modern patriarchal religious convention.

The figure of a frog and a red stoneware pot in the shape of a woman both remind me of Mayahuel's endless capacity for transformation and sustenance. The fish sign of the Christians has new meaning for me as Mayahuel's fish son. His dismemberment, a primordial version of the crucifixion, but unrelated to the concept of sin, helps me to open more softly to the Christian story. (See also stories of Sedna, Isis, Juno, and Shapash.)

The Story That
Never Ends

o you want to hear the story that never
ends? Yes? Yes! Here is the story that never
ends.

Out of the four hundred bloody
mouths of the frog goddess Mayahuel
came all the creatures of the world. And then Mayahuel, endlessly
bleeding one, took up her jeweled green frog skin and made of it a band
for the sand-white garment her woman form would wear. Into that
dress she stepped, and into her nose she fastened a plate of blue. Into
her hair the color of flames she bound the feathers of the eagle. Their
soft points sprang out about her face like the rays of the sun.

Then into the waters at her feet she looked and showed her teeth
with pleasure. She saw she was supple as a tongue and lovely as a dewy
night under the full of the moon. She called then, sweet and throaty, to
Snake-the-Wind, singing and crooning, holding her breasts and whispering his name.

"Beautiful Ehecatl," sang the goddess Mayahuel. "Blow to me, bend to me, my treasure, my Wind."

Snake-the-Wind quickened when he heard the voice of his beloved. His nostrils opened and his lips parted. With lithe fingers, he clothed his wind self in the skin of the snake. His chest swelled. He bent and he blew.

"Ehecatl!" the voice of Mayahuel was thin with joy.

"Mayahuel, I come!" The voice of Snake-the-Wind was gigantic with hope. He slithered and surged. Mayahuel knelt and rocked. When Snake-the-Wind arrived, he slipped himself between her elbows and her waist and wrapped himself about her swaying back. The eyes of Mayahuel and Snake-the-Wind sang to each other a thousand hymns. The tips of the tongues of Mayahuel and her Wind-Snake touched. Ehecatl bit the shoulder of his goddess, and Mayahuel took his long and lovely length into her arms.

Out of the union of Mayahuel and Ehecatl was born a son in the shape of a fish. To birth this son, Mayahuel breathed and moaned, and Ehecatl rubbed sweet oil into her belly and then caught the child that plunged gleaming from her center.

Then, to suckle her water child, she grew four hundred woman breasts where the four hundred mouths of her frog self had been. Now the endlessly bleeding one was the endlessly milking one, and the fish son's skin grew fat and orange with health.

Surely this son had come to magnify life's abundance, for no matter the cares of his thousand questions or his busy interruptions to their love, the child brought to Mayahuel and Ehecatl a joy that deepened as he grew.

It came to pass that this well-beloved son of the endlessly milking one and Snake-the-Wind took the form of a boy. How the mother and father cherished this child with his snapping eyes and soft mouth that told them stories! For the fish boy son had begun to travel, staying in the homes of the creatures of the world, listening to them and taking his impressions as a creature himself. And so the innocence of his infanthood peeled away, leaving in its place a wisdom colored with energy and tinged with sadness.

One evening when the shadows were long, Mayahuel caught a look on the fish son's face that filled her with a kind of dread. She saw that his was the face of a boy no longer. His was the face of a man now, at the same time restless and peaceful with purpose.

Mayahuel hovered at the edge of the dark, swollen with feeling.

"It is the creatures," said her son, in answer to her query. "I am come that they might have life, and have it more abundantly."

Mayahuel felt a thread of relief inside her. "They have that in you, Son. They have that in you. You inspire them. Their lives are richer, I know, for your visits and your stories."

Fish Son turned to look at his mother, and his eyes were very kind. "I have the gift of stories, Mother," he said. "But inspiration is not enough when the creatures are hungry. I have also the gift of green, Mother. And I must give that, too."

Mayahuel felt her throat tighten. The relief had fled. "How will you do that, my son?" she whispered.

Fish Son reached out his hands to his mother's. She took them in her own. Both their eyes were swimming with tears.

"I will take fish form again, Mother. And I will lie out of the water and I will die. Then you will cut me in pieces and bury me. And then I will come to you and the creatures in a new form."

Mayahuel felt the mouths of her frog self loosen inside her. She saw the dress of her woman self muddy and torn. She felt the shrivel of her four hundred breasts, and she let her son take her into his arms.

"It is good that you didn't argue with him," said Snake-the-Wind. And the mother and father clung to each other until the morning came.

When Fish Son died, the goddess Mayahuel made of her four hundred breasts four hundred eyes. She cut up and buried her beautiful son and watered his grave with a river of tears.

From Fish Son's body deep in the wet earth sprang up seed-bearing plants for the creatures of the world. From his hair came cotton; from his nostrils the herb for curing fevers. From his toes came the sweet potato, and out of his knees grew the maize. Indeed, to a thousand times four hundred, Fish Son's body made all of the fruits and grains of this world. The creatures of the world rejoiced and gave thanks over and over again for the gift of green.

Then the goddess Mayahuel closed her four hundred eyes and began to sing the song of the story that never ends. She sang it round and round and formed of herself the maguey plant, a deep green cactus shrub with four hundred hard, pointed leaves in a rosette spiral. Into the plant she poured herself; into its blossom she hummed the love of herself and her Ehecatl. "Neither drought nor hail nor cold touch us here, my beloved," she sang. And she filled herself with the wine of her endless milking.

Endlessly milking is Mayahuel to this very day. When under her the creatures of the world put their pots, storing her milk for the pulque of intoxication and blessing, they hear (yes they do!) in her voluminous white essence the story that never ends.

Spider Grandmother

Kiowa

Introduction

S pider Woman of the North American Pueblo peoples, whose threads were said to descend into the small doors atop her people's heads if they but remembered to keep them open, may be more than coincidentally related to the Kiowan's Spider Grandmother. Both images honor the fascinating arachnid whose tiny size belies her silent power to create, preserve, and destroy from the center of her web.

Spider Grandmother is not precisely a goddess figure. She is, however, like Baubo and Hecate (see stories), a precise image of the old woman who is, in turn, an image of the crone aspect of the great feminine. In the culture of control, both spider and old woman are stepped on and maligned. Despite the spider's vital role as insect predator and her remarkable role as weaver, she regularly draws revulsion. Likewise, the vast knowledge, wisdom, and persistance of the old woman is rendered invisible, ridiculed, scorned, or vilified. Both spider and old woman lie powerfully in our own psyches, waiting quietly to help us find our own suns.

Kiowan women, once part of the largest tribe of nomadic peoples on the North American plains, and today living in the midst of Oklahoma, once participated in neither government nor hunt. Like spiders spinning, they performed the endlessly repetitive tasks that allowed larger dramas to unfold. Perhaps the Kiowan storyteller compensated for the glorification of male drama-makers by making a hero of Spider Grandmother. This tale is retold from the one in Merlin Stone's *Ancient Mirrors of Womanhood*.

Spider makes her delicate web with undivided persistence. If she missteps, she simply pauses, and then continues, not tearing her errors down, but simply incorporating them. She grows by shedding her rigid, outer shell. She pulls loose part by part, weak at first, but soon hardens the firm exoskeleton from which to move again. I'm convinced she has arms, not legs, and waves at me knowingly as I, too, over and over, climb out of and into the skins of my life.

Spider Grandmother Finds Light for Her People

very long time ago, the world was young. There was no light. It was night all the time, even in daytime. One dark day, the animals gathered together to complain. "We must have light!" they told one another. "We can't see anything—not even the ground we walk on."

Rabbit held up his foot. "Don't worry any longer," he said. "I will find light." So away Rabbit hopped to find light. But he came back with nothing.

Fox shoved his way to the center of the crowd. "Our people have nothing to fear," said Fox. "The great Fox is here! I will find light." Then Fox strode off to find light. But Fox came back with his head low. He, too, had not been able to find light.

Then Eagle drew himself up to his full height. When he spoke, all the other animals were quiet. "I will bring my people light," said Eagle. And he soared away on his great wings. But Eagle came back with his wings drooping in discouragement. Eagle could not find light either.

Woodpecker thought he would try his luck. "I-I-I ca-ca-ca-cacan f-f-f-f-find lie-lie-lie-light," said Woodpecker. But Woodpecker returned as the others had, without light.

The animals continued to complain and brag among themselves. Then suddenly, they heard a tiny voice that sounded very old. "I believe I can bring light to our people," said the voice.

"Who's that?" shouted Fox.

"Yesssss, who ssssssaid that?" asked Snake.

"It's Spider Grandmother!" guffawed Fox, slapping his knee.

Eagle put up his wing to hide his beak. Then he threw back his head and laughed. "If even I can't find light, how does Spider Grandmother think she can?" he chortled.

The other animals snickered and chuckled. "Spider Grandmother? Ha! She's too little, and she's way too old."

Well, Spider Grandmother had lived a very long time and she was very wise. So it wasn't that she didn't hear the animals laughing at her. She did hear them. She just didn't pay them much attention.

Instead, she set out on a journey to the land of the sun people. She crossed vast deserts. She climbed up high mountains and down their other sides. She walked around huge lakes. All the while she walked, she spun out her thread behind her, so that she would be able to find her way back to her people. She traveled through the dark of many days and the dark of many nights. Once she stopped to make a bowl of some cool clay she had found. Then, carrying her bowl, she pushed on, spinning her thread behind her and moving closer and closer to the land of the sun people.

Finally, Spider Grandmother saw an orange glow at the edge of the darkness. It began to turn pink, and Spider Grandmother knew then that she had arrived in the land of the sun people. Closer and closer she crept to the huge fire that lit the land of the sun people. Then quickly and quietly, so quickly and quietly that none of the sun people noticed her, Spider Grandmother broke off a piece of the fire, put it in her bowl, and began to follow her thread back to her people.

To her surprise, however, the fire in the bowl began to grow. It grew bigger and bigger, and hotter and hotter. It got so hot and so big that Spider Grandmother could stand it no longer. So, small as she was, she hurled the fire into the sky, so high that it stuck. And there it stays to this day, where it is the sun that lights our days.

But Spider Grandmother remembered to save a tiny piece of the fire in her bowl. That piece she took back to her people. That is how the people got fire to cook their food, to bake their bowls hard, and to light their campfires at night.

And that is why, to this very day, when people sit around their campfires at night, they tell stories, like this one, about Spider Grandmother.

VII

Recovery of Herstory

A cquiring knowledge of personal history is life changing. It shifts attitude, action, and even circumstance: things are never the same again. The puzzle finally fits together when the secrets are revealed. Adopted child meets birth mother. The "big brother" is really the father and "mama" is really the grandmother. The meaning of the lifelong nightmare is the childhood sexual abuse she never remembered until now. The "nervousness" is really mental illness; the "bad moods" are really alcoholism. The "terrible shame" is actually a first divorce or a baby "out of wedlock." Whether the news is good or bad, we are relieved. The gnawing feeling that the story as told just does not make sense falls away. The truth is out; we are whole.

Like secrets in an individual family, our collective herstories have been hidden from us. The "photos" destroyed; "family" mythologies doctored; the "documents" altered and even completely rewritten. The commonly taught western history, for example, that humankind leapt from cave to the biblical era to Greece in a continuous stream of patriarchally dominated culture is a colloquial lie so pervasive that it is hard to ascribe ill will to it. After all, one historian simply starts where another leaves off, and no one, until the likes of Riane Eisler, Marija Gimbutas, Barbara Mor, Monica Sjoo, Merlin Stone, and Barbara Walker have questioned the assumptions or "facts" of this story. On the contrary, like children who repress hunches and inconsistencies in family mythology, historians and their publics have swallowed facts that are not facts and interpretations that rob us of our ability to know who we are.

Western "history" has long explained ancient Europe as a land of barbarians until the Greeks rose up out of the historical void. Actually, Europe was in large part peopled with women and men who together created civilizations focused on art, trade, agriculture, and architecture.

From the ruins and artifacts of their cities, we know these people neither expected nor perpetrated war; they valued the creative and worshipped the goddess. As long ago as seven thousand years before what we accept as the Common Era, ancient European civilizations honored life in a way we are both shocked and thrilled to learn. We are shocked that we have not been told. How could they pretend that men have always dominated? Why did they not tell us that matrifocal civilizations fell at the hands of patriarchal invaders, who then borrowed their knowledge while degrading their lands and rewriting their records? The lies, we find, also blanket the "Middle Ages." Women were healers, then, burned by the millions as witches in order that male doctors co-opt their knowledge, take their lands, and rewrite their records. The story of the burning times has been silenced; only in the code of fairy tales in which witches are alive, but demonic, can we glimpse the power once held by women spiritually connected to earth.

We are shocked, stung in a way that even all our cynicism and sophistication will never completely heal. But we are also thrilled. We are living in the times when the secrets are out. We are naming them, touching them alone and together. We are closing our eyes and letting our bones tell us what it must have been like. Suddenly the dropped stitches are picked up again. We are finding her image and presence in every country, every continent. We are telling herstory: we are telling our stories. Our hearts, afraid for the future, are madly borrowing hope from the past.

Lilith, Lady of the Air

(LILL-ith)

Middle East

Introduction

R elated to the Sumerian goddess Ninlil, lady of the air who gave birth to the moon, Lilith, hand of Inanna (see story), is identified with the lily or lotus. The lily is the great mother's flower *yoni,* which begets herself and the world (see stories of Juno and Astarte). The sweeping sexuality of her person characterizes the endless mysteries of growing things over which she once unquestionably ruled. Her powers, however, were politically unacceptable to the nomadic tribes who coveted the fields of her farming peoples. The nomadic story-tellers, therefore, invented a degrading biography for the lady of the moon.

Except inasmuch as her image was collapsed into that of Lucifer, the goddess Lilith lost her place entirely in the Christian Bible. In both Eve and the serpent, biblical writers subverted images of the creator goddess honored by earlier Middle Eastern creation myths. In Eve, they reduced the one who is complete to wife of the first man, subordinate and obedient, experiencing sexuality for procreative purposes only. The snake, who possesses the secret of the tree of knowledge, is a disguised and diabolized version of the goddess herself.

Rabbinical writers, on the other hand, retained the divine lady in the form of the night hag in the mystical book of the Kabbalah (see story of the Shekina). They wrote Lilith herself into the script—as Adam's first wife. She refuses to do Adam's bidding, however, and flies away when he insists that she forego her ancient position of pleasure and lie beneath him. While Yahweh creates Eve, Adam's second wife, in this story, Lilith takes the form of a she-demon who spends her evenings in the beds of dreaming men, milking them for nightly ejaculate and making of their sperm a hundred new demons a day. Beautiful temptress she is, they tell us, with long waving hair and claws for feet, like a bird of prey (see story of Cerridwen).

It is easy to see Eve and Lilith as two sisters, both degraded versions of the goddess, who, split from each other, represent two halves of a once-sacred sexual whole. Eve is the sister of pregnancy and motherhood; Lilith is the sister of menstruation and independence. Integrated, they represent a body of wisdom that scorns the intellectualization of truth. Penelope Shuttle and Peter Redgrove have helped me to understand the connection of Eve and Lilith in their book, *The Wise Wound: Menstruation and Everywoman.*

Lilith's story here is a kind of political cartoon. It plays with the biblical Genesis 1 story of Adam's naming of the creatures. The preachers of my childhood never failed to interpret this as Yahweh's setting of humans superior to all other life. Now, I am the first person to name things. This whole book is about naming. But this story functions to balance my urgency about having to know through analysis, discrimination, and hierarchical thinking. It balances that sly tendency of the intellect to believe that because it thinks, I am. Lilith, for me, is about an is-ness I find as elusive but powerful as a dream of flying.

The First Woman
and the Gift of the Moon

n the beginning was the woman Lilith and
the man Adam. They were wife and husband and lived in a garden called Eden.
The garden was so green it rested the eyes
like a cool cloth. Its fruits were as many as
the stars of the sky. Together Lilith and Adam grew to know the plants
and animals they lived with and to lie together, quiet and joyful, under
the whispering trees.

But one day Adam took an idea into his head. "Lilith," said Adam,
"It's not enough to know our plants and animals. Let's name them in
order to separate them from each other."

Lilith stretched. The snake at her side entwined itself in her reaching
arms.

"Seems like we're all just fine here without names," said Lilith. She
yawned.

But Adam sat up. He liked his new idea, and he began to spend whole days comparing sounds for the creatures. "His creatures," he began to call them. Every day he paced and thought and named animals.

Soon he added plants. So absorbed was he, that he grew away from lying with Lilith, sometimes spending the whole night at his new project.

One day Adam said to Lilith, "Lilith, have you ever noticed how big I am? See, I'm much bigger than you." Adam showed his muscles. "Look how tall I am."

Lilith looked quietly at Adam. The snake curled silent beside her.

"Lilith, I'm going to call myself king." said Adam. "King of this garden."

The snake uncoiled and undulated into the bush.

"I don't like the sound of that, Adam," said Lilith.

"It doesn't really matter if you like the sound, Lilith," said Adam. "I am the biggest and the strongest. So you've got to do what I say."

"There are other ways to measure bigness than in inches, and other ways to measure strength than in muscles," said Lilith.

"Oh, come on, Lilith," said Adam. "If I'm the king, then you're my queen."

"No, thanks," said Lilith. She stood up. "We're all sisters and brothers in this garden. Each of us is as important as the other. Nobody's king and nobody's queen."

Adam didn't listen, so Lilith walked away. Finally, one day, when Adam started the argument again, Lilith sat for a long time and watched the snake seem to die, wither and shrivel its skin, and then slide taut and glistening into its life.

That was the day Lilith took herself out of the garden. Through its gates she went and into the netherworld. There she sat still and quiet in the dark.

Adam was so furious at Lilith's leave-taking that even when he married the woman Eve and had a family of children, he continued to fume against her. "Snake lover!" he spat. "Not a woman, but a demon!"

"Hush, Adam!" said Eve. "Not in front of the children!"

Lilith alone in the Netherworld grew large. She was going to have a child. Waiting for the child, she gathered a gift to give to the sons and daughters of Adam and Eve. To a girl and a boy sleeping deep in a field she sent the dream of farming.

Soon after that dream was dreamed by the girl and the boy, Lilith had her child. On a black night at the edge of the sea, hanging hard to the dark with her hands and pushing against it with her feet, Lilith gave birth to the moon.

Astarte, the Guiding Star

(uh-STAR-tay)

Middle East

Introduction

To the Semites of Canaan, Mesopotamia, and Arabia, lands we now call Lebanon, Israel, Syria, and Iraq, the goddess Astarte was queen of heaven. Some of the earliest written material ever found details her worship in periods that predate and coincide with biblical sagas. The judges and prophets of Old Testament stories repeatedly call for her destruction. Their diatribes suggest that the Hebrews, often thought to be a homogeneous group, were actually a combination of roving tribes and settled cities, only some of whom were willing to adopt one sky god over the mother of all *baalim,* or gods.

The judge Jeremiah, for example, records the Hebrew women's rage and sorrow against the suppression of worship of their Guiding Star. They take to the streets, shouting. Famine and want have followed her cancellation, they chant. But Jeremiah, fist raised, admonishes them that the real cause of the current agricultural disaster is the people's refusal to worship Yahweh.

The story clearly suggests that natural calamity abetted the repression of the goddess, both by physically weakening her worshippers and by creating in them the psychology of despair that can so easily shift allegiance. The children of Israel had built shrines to the queen of heaven in city towers, on hills, in groves, and under every green tree. But Yahweh-worshipping Hebrews invaded their neighbors under orders from their lord to "utterly destroy all the places . . . to break in pieces the images and cut down the groves, and fill those places with the bones of men" (Deuteronomy 12:2–3; 2 Kings 23:14). The Israelite queen Maacah was dethroned for worshipping the lady in a grove (1 Kings 15:13).

Called Athtar, Attar, Attart, and Ishtar, Astarte is one of the oldest forms of the goddess in the Mideast (see stories of Shapash, and Inanna and Ereshkigal). The same creating, preserving, destroying goddess worshipped by all Indo-European cultures, she was related to Hathor, Isis, Urania, Demeter, and Aphrodite. Mother of All Souls, Astarte ruled over the spirits of the dead who, with the light of heaven for their robes, took the form of stars. Associated with the sea and the serpent, and ancient prototype of the Virgin Mary, Astarte's sacred drama in Syria and Egypt reenacted the rebirth of the solar god from this celestial virgin every December 25 (see stories of Juno Lucina and Mary). Symbol of her ability to regenerate herself as the world, her lily is the same as the lily-lotus of Juno and Lilith (see stories). Northern Europeans called her Ostara or Eostre, from which her sacred "Easter lilies" are derived.

Astarte's *yoni* or sacred vulva was also represented by the Hebrew word *hor*—synonymous with hole, cave, or pit, and fascinating cognate for the degraded English word *whore*—representing both the goddess herself and her priestesses, by whose sexual rituals the unclean could purify themselves. Diving into the pool of water in the sanctum of her temple symbolized the sexual intercourse by which a man could realize *horasis* or spiritual enlightenment (very likely a precursor to the rite of baptism). Modern scholars, schooled in the concept that sexuality is at best simply a matter of physical fertility, have misnamed the hundreds of images of Astarte they have found buried by her worshippers in the earth. Calling them "fertility figures" misrepresents Astarte Quadesh, that which is holiness. Tireless guide of humankind, lady of the lands, the goddess Astarte was none other than sovereign of the world.

I wrote Astarte's story as an antidote to the painful series of Bible stories in which worshippers of "idols" are murdered and their cities, animals, and crops burned. At a living room ritual honoring the buried parts of ourselves, we each molded her image out of clay—then sang, talked, and ate together while her small selves baked in the kitchen.

The Burning
of the Lady's People

ama, why are the stars cold?" Sal asked his mother one afternoon as she ground meal for bread. Sal had carried a pot of water from the well at the city square, and now he sat down in the shade of the porch near his mother and baby sister, who slept in a basket nearby.

"I don't think they are cold, little lamb," said his mother. "I think they just seem cold because they're so far away. But you know what they really are?"

"What?" said Sal.

"They're all the children of the Guiding Star, our Astarte," said Sal's mother.

"The stars are her babies?" asked Sal.

"Yes," said his mother. "They're all the spirits of the people ever in the world—before they are born and after they die."

"Is Grandma a star then?" asked Sal.

"Yes, and you were a star before you came to live with me and Daddy."

"Was Sister too?" said Sal.

"Yes," said his mother.

Sal was quiet. Then he said, "Mama."

His mother looked up. She stopped grinding meal. "What, Sal?" she asked.

"Mama, if Daddy gets killed will he turn into a star?"

"Yes, sweetheart," said his mother, and she opened her arms. Sal went to stand inside her hug. "But, Sal, I think Daddy's going to come home safe for us," she whispered.

Sal lived thousands of years ago in a big city in a land called Canaan. Sal's family and all the other families in that city worshipped the great mother Astarte. Astarte's big temple sat at the center of the city, and every home held a little altar for Astarte right next to the oven where they baked their bread. Each family kept beautiful things on its altar: weaving and fruits and a small clay figure of Astarte in the shape of a mother with a baby inside her. Sal's daddy said that was to remind the people that Astarte was always making new life. Sal's mother said Astarte never slept and she helped life grow and she also made dying. It was like a big circle, his mother said. Being born, growing, getting old, and dying, and then back to being born again.

This was a frightening time for the people in Sal's city. Sal's daddy and a lot of other boys and men had marched out of the city in an army. When Sal asked his father why, his daddy said it was because the invaders were coming.

"What's invaders?" asked Sal.

"They're people who want our land," said Sal's father.

"Why?" said Sal.

"I don't know," said his father. "But Daddy's going to make sure you and Mama and Sister are safe."

"When will you come back, Daddy?" asked Sal.

"As soon as I can," said his father.

It seemed to Sal that his daddy was gone a very long time. Then one day, Sal and his friends were playing sticks at the gate to the city. Suddenly, a boy said, "Hey! Look!" When the others looked, they could see a cloud of dust in the distance.

"It's Daddy!" said Sal. "Maybe the army's back!"

The children didn't play anymore. They just watched the cloud of dust puff bigger and bigger. When they could see people in the distance, they began to run toward them.

The men waved when they saw the children, but there were so many of them that the children, instead of trying to find their own brothers and fathers and uncles, raced back to the gates of the city. Shouting the news, they ran through the streets.

"They're home!" yelled Sal. "Mama, Mama, Daddy's coming!"

Sal's mother got tears in her eyes. She hugged Sal hard.

Sal's little sister clapped her hands and crowed.

"Mama, Mama, come on! He's almost here!" Sal pulled on his mother's arm.

Sal's mother kissed Sal's head. "Lamb, he won't come here right away," she said.

"Mama, why? He's home," said Sal.

"I know, Sal, but first he must go to the temple."

"Why?" asked Sal.

"Well, for Daddy to come back and eat with us and love us and live with us, he has to get the war and fighting off him," said his mother.

"How, Mama?" asked Sal.

"Well, Astarte's priestesses will take away his war clothes and bathe him and feed him holy food and hug him and sing to him. Then they will give him home clothes and he can come back to us," said his mother.

Sal's little sister crawled across the floor and a neighbor burst into the room. "They're home, Rebia!" she said to Sal's mother. "Did you see your daddy, Sal?" she asked.

Sal stopped. "No, but he's coming," Sal said.

"Sal!" said his mother. Her voice sounded high and anxious. "I thought you said you saw him!"

"I saw them, Mama," said Sal. "I know he's coming."

Well, Sal was right. The days it took seemed very long, but Sal's daddy did return home. He gathered Sal and his mother and little sister into his arms and held them all very close. "How I've missed you!" he said, and wiped away his tears.

"Daddy!" said Sal. "Did you kill the invaders?"

"No, Son," said his father. "There are many, many invaders, and they move in small groups, so they are hard to find."

Sal's little sister gurgled, and Sal climbed on his daddy's lap.

"Rebia," said Sal's father to his mother. "The invaders are burning whole cities."

Sal's mother picked up her little girl. Sal could see that his mother's eyes were frightened.

"People say that the invaders have a god that wants all the land."

"And the people on the land?" whispered Sal's mother.

"It's bad, Rebia," said Sal's daddy.

Sal looked at his parents' faces, trying to understand.

"Daddy, why?" said Sal. "Why can't they share the land? Why can't we all live here?"

"Sal, that's a very good question. And I don't know the answer," said his father. "Rebia, I want us to bury our Astarte."

Sal's little sister began to cry. Sal's mother's lips turned very pale. "What are you thinking?" she asked.

"Rebia, I'm thinking that no matter what happens, I want to save the idea of our great mother," said Sal's father.

That night Sal's family stayed very close together. After they ate, Sal's mother and father dug a hole next to the oven. Sal got to put the little figure of the mother with the baby inside her into the ground and help press dirt on top of her. Sal's mother many times chanted the name Astarte and some other words Sal couldn't understand.

"Daddy?" asked Sal. "Why doesn't Astarte want all the land, like the invaders' god?"

"Sal, Astarte is the land," said Sal's father. "She is all the animals and all the plants and all the waters and all the sky. She is the soil and the wind."

"And the stars too?" asked Sal.

"The stars too," said his father.

The invaders did not come right away. But they did come.

And they burned the city Sal lived in and all its people.

Why? you might ask.

It's very hard to understand, and we don't really know the answer to that question. But Sal's father had a good idea when he buried the figure of Astarte. There have been many invaders and many wars since that time so long ago. Many people have lived and died, and many people have hurt the earth because they did not know about Astarte.

But not so long ago, people began to find little figures of Astarte deep in the ground in the place where Sal's city stood so long ago. "Who could this be?" they asked themselves. And slowly they pieced together the story of the great star mother.

"She's still here," they say to each other. "She's still here after all this time."

Lamia, Snake Woman

(LA-mee-uh)

Libya

Introduction

L amia is ancient as the snake herself in the desert–oasis land of Libya, once the name of all of northern Africa except for Egypt. Most probably she was worshipped by Libyan-Berber peoples, a light-skinned, nomadic group of Africans whose descendants still herd camels, goats, and sheep in the Sahara and the mountainous areas of Algeria, Morocco, and Tunisia. Associated historically with the ancient goddess-worshipping Amazons of Herodotus's history, the Berbers today are connected with North Africa's Tuareg people. The position of the Tuareg woman is unique in the Islamic world. Veilless, she is able to demand monogamy and divorce. She marries relatively late, and enjoys an unguarded sexual life prior to marriage. Guardian of tradition, she writes tribal script, keeps alive legend, myth, and song, and is expert user of herbal cures. Succession is through her line, rather than her husband's.

The ancient Greeks were greatly influenced by the Libyans. They borrowed Lamia for stories of their own making, stories that not so much stripped the goddess of her power, but eroded the people's relationship with her so that it no longer challenged them to probe her endlessly renewing mystery. Medusa is the Greek name for Lamia; the serpent goddess is known too as Neith, Athene, Anatha, Buto, and, in ancient Babylonia, Lamashtu. Called mother of gods, daughter of heaven, and great lady, her name was used in the European Middle Ages as a general term for witch or demon in the shape of woman. (See story of Lilith.)

I collect and write the stories in this book in the context of a patriarchy under increasing pressure to change. The stories are also branded with my reaction to my fundamentalist Christian background and my intense interest in feminism, spirituality, and mythology itself. Historically, tellers of the story of the snake goddess Lamia were similarly affected by cultural pressures, personal histories, and particular audiences. The story of Lamia in this collection is my version of how their versions perhaps developed.

All powerful archetypes undergo tremendous change as current cultural forces shape them. We may glimpse the power the goddess once held just by observing the breadth and depth of changes wrought on her mythologies. Changes in the story of the snake woman goddess are particularly exemplary. The snake, once unquestionably revered, underwent a stunning reversal of status. From reverence to revulsion, from mystery to mockery she fell. Only forces of disrespect, misuse, and cruelty could have been at work in the lives of people who began to view the snake's transforming power as evil rather than awesome.

Pictures and readings about the snake can invoke Lamia. This goddess in my life is the agony and beauty of changing slowly and absolutely.

How the People of
Today Have Two Stories

ver since the beginning, fear of Lamia, the snake woman, has coiled in the bellies of all who sense her majesty and mystery. She may be tensed and swaying, upright in readiness. She may unhinge her jaws and swallow a fat and complex life into her own thin, simple length. We watch her, and our fingernails dig into the soft flesh of our palms. And when she lies white as death, with eyes blind and darting tongue still, our own eyes turn deep into the unanswered, and we are afraid. We look in wonder when she climbs without arms or legs from her dull and brittle coat into the new one soft and vividly colored. We are relieved. She is alive. We are full of hope. She returns again. But we feel afraid. Yes, with Lamia, snake woman of the deepest dance we know, we are a little afraid. It has always been so!

It was so with the first people. They were the people of the limitless dunes at the edge of the stunning blue sea, the people of the cliffs bordering the dry rivers. They were the people who copied their snake woman to receive the gift of the oasis.

There in the land where the wind blows in yellow pillars and the heat is cruel, the first people in the desolate morning formed a great circle with snake woman at their center. They held hands and danced to the drums that copied the slow beat of Lamia's heart. The first people's dance was measured, and snake woman, head and neck hidden by a cloth, sang and swayed at the center.

"Who are you, Lamia?" the first people called to her, wondering and afraid, pitching their voices low and simple as the body of the snake at the center.

"Copy me and you shall see," answered Lamia.

The first people of Lamia copied her deadness. They unhinged their jaws to mimic her swallowing of life. They lay without moving or moaning. "You are like the ghibli winds," they sang to her. "You leave nothing living, not even the fetus in the mother's womb."

The people copied Lamia new and large and young again. "You are like the winds of the north," they crooned. "Your waters draw shrubs from the earth for our sheep to feed on. You make us fertile, you make us virile, you fill our children with strength."

The first people paced out her rhythm again and again, smoldering, undulating, bodies and voices turning in exhausted circles, slinking toward the afternoon.

"Who are we, Lamia?" the people sang.

"Copy me and you shall see," answered snake woman.

The people trickled out their sound and their sweat. Their feet and their hair turned hot and limp. And when the sun stood finally at the bottom of the sky, the desert blossomed.

The dunes were dahlia red, the sand floor mustard yellow. The hills turned coral and violet.

"She is the deep and the wet one."

It has always been so!

"She is the necklace of life under the sand."

It has always been so!

"We are the jewel keepers."

"We are the builders of the vats."

It will always be so!

When the dark came, then, the sky blazed with stars, the drums grew silent, and Lamia's people dreamed of plumbing the underground water for the figs, palms, oranges, pomegranates, and almonds of the oasis.

Lamia's first people drew from the basin of her rocks her water gift. From those precious wells came the moisture to grow the barley, the wheat, the millet, the onions, and the tomatoes beside the skeletons of riverbeds and streams. The size of the oasis grew by trees, and in gratitude and wisdom her first people continued to copy her rhythm.

One day it happened that a ship blew from the north over the sea. The ship, bound for trading with the people of Lamia, carried on it a sailor who entertained his brothers with stories he wove from the boredom and novelty of his adventures. The teller's words were quick as a child's who comforts himself in the midst of fear.

Orestes, the teller, was a small, sweet-eyed man with a scurrying gait. His hands busied themselves with carving or smoking or mending, and he asked his audience often, "Do you know what I mean?" His listeners said yes! and encouraged him to continue.

The words of Orestes were fantastic, enchanting, and tragic. His tales could drive away hunger, shorten the night, and take the pain out of a lashing. Stories and mead, Orestes said: both numb the agonies.

Orestes told of slaves yoked neck to neck, herded bare of foot over sharp rocks, the dead and ill cut away at night and left to make mountains of skulls at the crossings of the roads. Paradise, said Orestes, was a cave rained over by a veil of tears. Like crystals, you could look through them and reach endlessly for what could have been but never will be.

Orestes told of the cave of the pythoness, the oracle at Delphi, who sees the future of kings in a cup of blood poured out of the moon and keeps her children in soft-shelled eggs under her heart. He told of ships that could fly and nectars shared by truced armies at banquets before the slaughters of betrayal began.

And privately, to his sad-eyed companion, the blond farmer boy with the tremulous, constant smile, the teller spoke of his mother, slave of the inner house, who nestled him sometimes and beat him at others, and whose food turned to poison if he tried to eat too much of it. Sometimes there were whippings that left him for dead.

"But all you can do," said Orestes, "is survive." He reached for the boy. "Do you know what I mean?"

The boy held Orestes in his rough young hands.

The day the ship docked on the northern coast of Africa, Orestes gave the boy his two gold coins for safekeeping. "You keep these so's I won't drink too much," he said. The two sailors went ashore to the traders' settlement at the edge of the land of the people of Lamia.

The keeper of the inn was a muscular man with blue veins twining his forearms when he lifted pots of stew in his kitchen. He liked the stories of Orestes and so let him sweep and wash the cooking pots in exchange for his supper and a jug of mead. In gratitude, Orestes borrowed the big man's tireless strength for the hero of the new stories that he spun for the innkeeper's customers.

Orestes and the boy did not sleep at the inn. They carried jug and blanket out under the dome of the sky. The sky here in this strange land was king; and in its giant starry blackness pulsed a peace that thickened and melted around the two sailors as they drank and held each other and finally slept.

On a blinding blue day that followed a night of stories and mead, Orestes and his friend discovered the oasis. Throbbing from the night's liquor, the man and boy walked in the searing heat until they came upon that place of green and water. Here, in this infernal land, was shade and rest. And possibly more mead, thought Orestes, to mend this morning's sickness.

But the sailors had come upon the people of Lamia who had begun her dance. Women and men alternating, holding hands, they circled slowly moving about the snake at the center.

The sailors stared. Head and neck covered by a cloth, this center snake raised herself upright, now coiling and swaying, now still again. The white sky pounded in the sailors' heads with the drum from the heart of the circle. In and out people moved, close now, back, close again, sweat pouring down their faces and sides. Slowly, out and in, facing this snake, pacing a pattern on the sand, the circle slithered and twisted.

Orestes felt his head reel. The snake at the center became like woman to him, alive now and beautiful, then dead and unreachable. The dancers were the snakes now, twisting and ancient, lethargic as water, turning endlessly around this lunging, quiet beauty at the center who held the people to her bottomless flow of movement. Orestes and the boy could not understand the language of the people of Lamia. They could not know that her people gained her strength by imitating her, that they found her answers by taking her shape. Orestes and the boy could not understand the slowness of this dance. Their own people's dances were speedy and wild.

Something terrified stirred in Orestes, and he began to shake. In the midst of the heat, his teeth chattered. The boy looked at the dancers and at the face of his friend. It was crumpled as a child's, and the boy, not smiling now, led Orestes by one chilled hand away from the oasis and back across the land to the sea.

The boy held Orestes on the sand. Orestes didn't know what had happened. He could only say how strange it was, women dancing with men that way, and the snake so pulsing at the center. "It was like a dream, do you know what I mean?" said Orestes. "Like a dream."

"Yes," said the boy. Seeing the snake made him think of the job he'd had lambing, where the newborns slipped into his hands, still connected to the ewes with cords like bloody snakes. He'd cut a cord when the throbbing stopped if the ewe couldn't bite through it herself.

"You feel scared when you do it," the boy said. "But it makes you feel good afterward. Seeing the lambs walking around, knowing they wouldn't if you hadn't helped."

The boy stretched his lips again in his lonely, trembling smile and Orestes held him now.

Because the snake woman stayed in the mind of Orestes, the storyteller, it so happened that Lamia, the wet one of the deep, became part of the stories of the land across the sea. But the storyteller knew neither her dance nor the power of copying her motions of life and death. Instead, he knew only the terrible fever cold that had swept him when he watched, ill from the night.

He had seen her power and was afraid, and so he made in his own language a story of a snake woman who terrorized and could be subdued only by the bravest of men.

And so it is to this day. We are the people with both stories. Like the slender shape of Lamia herself, our fear has followed the ripples of time, and we ask ourselves, as we have from the beginning, what to do with it. When we are the first people, we watch her and copy her. We learn and we are comforted. We keep the jewels of the oasis.

But when we are the people of Orestes, we have lost the jewels. The oasis lives only in our minds. There we crawl for comfort against the trampling and the slaveries. Now we are afraid of Lamia. We don't know to copy her. We try to control her instead.

In our fear there is power; in her power there is fear. Shall we copy her? Can we control her? We thirst and circle the winds in the deserts of our souls, wandering and wondering our dances of death and hope.

Saule, Mother and Daughter Sun

(sall)

Balts

Introduction

Present-day Latvians, Lithuanians, and Estonians—as well as the wholly assimilated Old Prussians—are the descendants of the Baltic peoples of ancient Northern Europe. Saule, the Baltic girl sun, inspired countless pieces of still-extant Baltic poetry and art. Called both *mate* for "mother" and *meita* for "daughter," Saule's imagery fills poem after psalm-like poem. She rides in a boat and chariot to the place in the invisible world where the dead continue to live, just as she herself shines through the night though we cannot see her. Baltic folklore—stories, songs, and proverbs—is one of the richest in all of Europe, revealing the ancient reverence for a world of living forests, hills, trees, springs, stones, and mountain slopes.

For more than two thousand years preceding the Christian crusades of the eleventh century C.E., the Balts worshipped the elemental world. For another four hundred years, country folk preserved their faith despite the strict outlawing of their rites and music by Christian nobility.

Jerome of Prague recorded in the early 1400s a Lithuanian tribal story of Saule's imprisonment in a tower by a powerful king. They worship the sun, wrote Jerome, and venerate the large iron hammer, forged by the signs of the zodiac, that broke open her jail.

The *zodiac*, which comes from the Greek for "living being," pictures the universe as a complete circuit or circle. Russian folklore preserves the sun as keeper of the twelve kingdoms, with the stars as her children. The twelve equal parts of the zodiac, each bearing the name of a constellation, correspond in astrology to the complexities of human experience.

To the seed of Jerome's story, I have added both Kalvaitis, the Baltic celestial blacksmith, counterpart of the Greek Haephestus, and the plot device of Saule's not having cried before being locked in the tower.

Saule, the girl sun, kisses our skins with her lips. Her tears, new in us again and again, wash us clean and open us to our skies.

The Sun, the Stars, the Tower, and the Hammer

aule, the sun, slips silently each day into the orchards of apples. There she loosens the silver brooches of her silky white shawl and hangs her scarlet belt on the oak at the center. The oak's leaves are silver, its gnarled branches copper, and its reaching roots iron. Saule dances in her silver shoes, red fern blossoms tucked in the twists of her braids. Her cheeks flame rosy as the apples as she sways and hops and rolls. Then, hair barely bound, blossoms littering the meadow, she rests, drinking up her liquid light from her round yellow jug.

Each evening, Saule journeys in her copper chariot away from the apple orchards, over the hills of silver, down to the edge of the sea. Into the waters she strides with her steeds, their hundred coats hot as fire but not sweating. Then she bathes them cool again, their golden reins hanging loose at their bridles. Finally, red crown glowing, she steps into her golden boat to sail beyond the hills of the souls to the center of the

240

world. There she sleeps in her castle coiled about with the eons and the days.

All day long, Saule presses her lips against the bare skins of those who pray to her. All the dead return to Saule, mother of life, who before she was locked in the tower had never cried.

No one knows quite how it happened. Some say a cruel king built a tower and locked Saule inside. Some say it was a queen, vexed with Saule's heat and power. Some say Saule went herself, out of curiosity, and the wind slammed shut the door and whirled away the key. However it happened, the structure had neither window nor crack, and its bricks were formed of darkness, its single door a slab of night.

Everywhere, the people mourned. Their light had fled, the golden boat submerged, the yellow jug cracked, and the apples gone soft and gray, fallen from the murky branches.

Even Kalvaitis, the smith of heaven, noticed the dark. A hush had fallen on the world. Kalvaitis, shut away in his tool-filled chambers, raining down sparks of silver upon the waters as he worked, noticed the strange silence when he rested from his crafts.

Then he heard a noise swell from below. People were shouting to the stars. "Bring back our sun!" they begged, voices full of fear and sorrow. "Bring back Saule!"

The constellations—ram, bull, twins, crab, lion, winged lady, scales, scorpion, archer, goat, water-bearer, and fish—heard the peoples' cry. Protectively, they circled the world, talking and arguing about the best way to help. Finally, they hit upon a plan. They went to the smith of heaven.

"We've come, Kalvaitis," said Aries the ram, "to help you make a hammer."

"A hammer?" asked the smith of heaven. "I have plenty of hammers."

"This hammer will be separate and different," said the ram, "from any ever seen before. It is a hammer to smash the tower that traps the sun."

"Ah!" said Kalvaitis. "So she is trapped! I thought I noticed that she was not here. In a tower, you say?"

"Built from earth to heaven," bellowed Taurus the bull. "And we've

241

no time to waste: the fruits are rotting in the fields, and no one can see to pick them." A vein bulged in the bull's neck. "I give your shoulders, Kalvaitis, extra strength for this forging."

The Gemini twins gestured with their four hands. "You'll need special materials," they intoned. "Body and mind, mortality and immortality, all and nothing. We'll blow our wind through your bellows."

Kalvaitis shook his head. "I thank you," he said. "I want to do this, I do. But I . . ."

"But you have so many other things to do," smiled Cancer the crab, feeling herself round and soft under her hard shell. "Kalvaitis, as a baby longs for mother's milk, may you long to make this hammer."

Leo the lion put a paw on Kalvaitis's heart. His mane bristled. "Kalvaitis, your hammer will break Saule's tower in just blows."

"But . . ." began Kalvaitis, "I need . . ."

"You need precision of timing," said Virgo, the lady with wings of wheat and corn. "I give you judgment and discipline strong as iron."

Libra the scales spoke evenly. "The halves of you—above and below, side and side—will flow together. Your work will be one with your idea."

The Scorpion laughed. "The work is essential. No doubt about it," she said. "But sleep, too, Kalvaitis! You must also sleep. I give you that sweet, mysterious dark. Renew yourself for the forging of Saule's hammer."

Kalvaitis bowed his head.

"I see you despairing of the responsibility," said Sagittarius the archer. She stretched up to reach Kalvaitis, her muscles taut. She touched him. "Do not fear. I fill you with optimism."

"And I," said Capricorn the goat, "fill you with just enough doubt to make you flexible. Plant your hooves, Kalvaitis—try again and then again!"

Aquarius, the long-haired boy with the giant urn, spoke next. "Here are the waters," he said, "to cool the hammer."

Kalvaitis clenched and unclenched his fists. Slowly, he looked from one constellation to the other.

Pisces the fish swayed gracefully. "We've given you our gifts, Kalvaitis," she said. "But you are the smith. We all know your compassion and imagination. That's why we came to you."

Everyone waited quietly. Then said Aries the ram, "We have spoken."

A great rummaging sound welled up as all the constellations—ram, bull, twins, crab, lion, winged lady, scales, scorpion, archer, goat, water-bearer, and fish—began to hum and shuffle. Kalvaitis closed his eyes. They circled around him, twinkling, touching him, and crooning him to sleep. The wheel of time turned itself backward and forward before Kalvaitis opened his eyes again and bent to his work. The stars hovered, winking at one another in satisfaction as they watched the smith of heaven wield intention, strength, tools, and skill.

Far away, Saule, locked in her tower, had been rocking, her face frozen. Suddenly, a strange water filled her eyes. The water spilled down her cheeks and a noise tore from her throat.

Kalvaitis merged air, metal, fire, and water.

Locked in the tower, Saule's tears came so freely that they washed hot around her feet. Swollen and exhausted though she was, tenderness and hope sparked within her.

Kalvaitis finished the hammer. His shoulders had been strong; the winds of his bellows mighty. The hammer was separate and different from any seen before.

Saule, in her tower, blind and deaf to the world without, felt her skin tingle with sudden expectation.

Kalvaitis swung the hammer. One! Two! The constellations hummed. Three!

With a roar and a whipping crash the neck of the tower broke, and Saule the sun burst from its shambles. She somersaulted. She soared.

The hillsides glinted again, tinting and elongating with color. The country folk flung open their doors and cavorted in the meadows.

Saule's hundred horses pranced and stamped. Tears slipped down her cheeks while she ran her hands over their flanks. She hitched them to her copper chariot and raced to her beloved apple orchards.

Saule cried for the wonderful open sky. She cried for the delicate silver leaves of the oak and the massiveness of its iron roots. She cried for the apples spoiled and shriveled on the ground. She filled the hill-sides with the red berries of her tears.

To this day, when Saule's people make pies and tarts of her apples and berries, they remember Saule's tears, the time of the tower, and the gifts of the stars. They remember the magic of the smith of heaven's hammer and that succulent, delirious moment of joy when Saule the sun spun free again.

Yemaya and Iamanja,
She Who Continues

(yeh-my-YAH and hee-ah-mansh-YAH)

Yoruba and Brazil

Introduction

Often depicted as a mermaid, fish mother Yemaya, goddess of the Ogun River and the sea, was worshipped by the Yoruba people of Nigeria who were enslaved by traders and carried in the stinking death holds of ships to the Americas. Sent by the thousands mainly from the cities of Ife and Benin—which had stood for four to five hundred years before the arrival of the Europeans in 1500—the Yoruba unwillingly settled British, French, Spanish, and Portuguese holdings in the "new world." There, to the present day, they have kept alive their pride and their goddess in Brazil, Cuba, Haiti, and Trinidad.

In Brazil, Yemaya is called Iamanja. She is a powerful sea mother, a Virgin Mary–like deity in the joyous Afro-Indo-Catholic religion in which rapturous, ecstatic dance and song summon her might, power, and mana.

Brazilian slaves and free blacks maintained ties with Africa almost entirely absent in the United States. For economic reasons, slave trade ended in the northern hemisphere by 1808. Subsequently, most North

245

American slaves were born in the United States, and memories of Africa grew dim. Slavery in Brazil, however, was not phased out until 1888, and crossings of blacks to Africa and back were frequent until 1905. *Malembos,* or friendships of solidarity and resistance among fellow captives, were nurtured by newcomers who spoke African languages and brought lifegiving myths and stories of home. *Malembos* enabled the rise of *quilombos* and *mocambos* (forest hideouts), found all over Brazil from the sixteenth century on. On the *quilombos,* fugitives could protest the system that bound them, return to a life free of a master's role, and practice African religions in freedom. Other slaves organized open resistance in the spirit of *malembo* or found ways to buy their freedom. Former Brazilian slaves often returned to Africa, sometimes to become important figures in society there.

Urban, rather than rural-dwelling, blacks in Brazil were most able to maintain African rites and customs, since they had the greatest freedom of movement and the strongest likelihood of meeting newly arrived slaves from their own nation who spoke their own language. To this day, Brazilians of many colors offer gifts of candles, food, perfume, flowers, and champagne to their great sea mother. On New Year's Eve, they wash away the impurities of the old year in the waters of Iamanja. On December 8, they honor her limitless mercy and protection. On the summer solstice, they float boats full of offerings on her waves. Bathers count seven swells in her name, reminiscent of the seven petticoats she is said to wear, before entering the sea. Fishermen call on her for protection for their precarious, raftlike vessels. Iamanja's color is blue.

Unlike the radical tampering endured by the Libyan goddess Lamia when her story survived the crossing to Greece (see story), the Nigerian water goddess Yemaya underwent changes that preserved her glory and comfort for the people who call her Iamanja in Brazil. Lamia's story was undoubtedly carried back to Greece by outsiders visiting Africa. Yemaya, on the other hand, became Iamanja when her people, victims of the slave trade, organized by the culture of control, brought her story themselves to the new continent. Tellers who thought they could gain from the patriarchy changed Lamia from wondrous to horrendous.

Iamanja's tellers had everything to gain by psychologically defending themselves against a way of life that had broken their connections with the land they called home.

I wrote the story of Yemaya and Iamanja to honor the organic process of change that stories undergo when their peoples change. It is also the story of people who mend the rents in the fabric of their lives with threads of rage, courage, love, and joy.

The Journey
to the New Land

hen we were the people of the round houses in the forests and the savanna, when our mornings were peopled with spirits, you, River Woman, Yemaya, were the flow that beat in our legs and hearts.

When time untwirled under Sky Keeper and clouds sang over the heat of your waters, you, Yemaya, floated and continued.

When Iron Maker cut the trees and we were the people in the square house kingdoms at the edge of the land, you, River Woman, widened your skirts and continued into the sea.

When we were the people who knelt to Allah in the afternoons, when we were the people who forgot your name, you, Yemaya, Sea Woman, continued.

When the bleached skins came and the stealing and selling of people began, when the screaming and whipped of the round houses were kicked to the coast to be branded and raped; when square-house people took money for the round-housers, when the wail tore from our guts, you, River to Sea, surged and continued.

When we were the people in chains, huddled against the nursing among us who soothed us, wounds and mouths, with milk; when we were the strangled and the starving and stood sobbing, you, Sea Woman, salted our tears and continued.

When the bleached skins jerked us to the prison boats and we, the people, took the journey of putrefaction, when we prayed to die, when we danced off the decks into your arms, you, Yemaya, endlessly swelling one, cold, clean, deep sleep, you continued.

When we were the people at the markets of the new coast, when the bleached skins had clothes and we could cover only our genitals, when we were taken sister from brother, mother from child, father from kin, when our livers were broken inside us, you, Lady of the Sea, Star of the River, you, Yemaya, continued to pulse.

When in the light and the air once again we could feel your sureness, when we wove a language of homes in this new place, when we called you Iamanja and dressed you in seven waves for petticoats, you, Star of the Sea, Lady of the River, drummed in our shoulders and feet.

When we were the people in the cities of the new land, when we moaned for the trees and curves of home, when we knew rage and sorrow like knives and bile in our throats, you called us to you, Iamanja, and continued.

When we were the ones who wanted to die, your waters carried to us new arrivals from our homes, new ones for us to care for and comfort, new ones with old stories of you in words that were lullabies in our ears and sweet home fruits in our mouths. When we would curse you and forget you, you continued, Lady of Compassion, you continued.

When the new ones' fury filled our spines with hope, when we planned and ran, when we made quilombos away from the masters, safe in the balmy woods, when we drank of you free and in peace far from the coasts of the new land, you blessed us, Lady of Purification, you continued.

When we braided you, Iamanja, Star of the Sea, with the Lady Maria of the cross and the spirits of the brown skins deep in the forests, when we knew you newer, wider, feasting, bathing, nesting us with the tender pride of the grandmothers we could never know, when you continued to undulate, Water Woman, our souls found a way to be quiet and dance.

When the rapes and the loves, Iamanja, made skins no more just black and brown and bleached, but all the shades between, when we were the people who bought our own freedom and the people who returned to the home of the beloved trees and curves, when the square-house people of Allah listened to our slave stories with shame and respect, when we became leaders in the old land, you, Protectress of Journeyers, you continued.

When we were the people the law loosed from bondage, you surged, Lady Maria, you continued.

When we were the people in the new land folding, like meat into broth, magic, desire, and passion into the worship of Maria, when we taught you could not enter us if we did not dance, when we said the bravest ones in the world are those who love, you, Iamanja, Mighty Woman of the Ebb, of the blind swaying plants, of the seven sacred petticoats, you continued.

When we are the sisters and brothers of the many skins who gather in a house, when we, coming together, break the shackles of the city and hoist you up to ride us, horses galloping through your waves, ride us, arms clinging, to meet ourselves, when we are the sweaters of ecstasy, the fish people of the deep, you, Queen of the River, Empress of the Sea, you of the flowers, the perfume, precious one, you continue to continue.

Book List

Adler, Margot. *Drawing Down the Moon*. Boston: Beacon Press, 1987.

Al-Anon's One Day at a Time. New York: Al-Anon Family Group Headquarters, Inc., 1978.

Al-Anon's 12 Steps and 12 Traditions. New York: Al-Anon Family Group Headquarters, Inc., 1984.

Bastide, Roger. *The African Religions of Brazil: Toward a Sociology of the Interpenetration of Civilizations*. Baltimore: Johns Hopkins Univ. Press, 1978.

Bernal, Martin. *Black Athena: The Afroasiatic Roots of Classical Civilization*. New Brunswick: Rutgers University Press, 1987.

Billington, James H. *The Icon and the Axe: An Interpretive History of Russian Culture*. New York: Random House, 1970.

Bowles, Paul. *Their Heads Are Green and Their Hands Are Blue: Scenes from the Non-Christian World*. New York: Ecco Press, 1963.

Bradshaw, John. *Healing the Shame that Binds You*. Deerfield Beach, FL: Health Communications, Inc., 1988.

Bolen, Jean Shinoda. *Goddesses in Everywoman*. San Francisco: Harper & Row, 1984.

_____. *Gods in Everyman*. San Francisco: Harper & Row, 1989.

Budapest, Zsuzanna. *Grandmother of Time*. San Francisco: Harper & Row, 1989.

Chatwin, Bruce. *The Songlines*. New York: Penguin Books, 1987.

Degler, Carl N. *Neither Black nor White: Slavery and Race Relations in Brazil and the United States*. New York: Macmillan, 1971.

Downing, Christine. *Journey Through Menopause*. New York: Continuum, 1989.

Duerk, Judith. *A Circle of Stones*. San Diego: LuraMedia, 1989.

Dworkin, Andrea. *Woman Hating*. New York: E. P. Dutton, 1976.

Erdoes, Richard, and Alfonso Ortiz. *American Indian Myths and Legends*. New York: Pantheon Books, 1984.

Farrar, Janet, and Stewart Farrar. *A Witches Bible Compleat*. New York: Magickal Childe, 1987.

_____. *The Witches' Goddess*. Seattle: Phoenix, 1987.

Freuchen, Peter. *Book of the Eskimos*. Cleveland: World Publishing Company, 1961.

Gadon, Elinor. *The Once and Future Goddess*. San Francisco: Harper & Row, 1989.

Gastor, H. Theodor. *The Oldest Stories in the World*. Boston: Beacon Press, 1952.

Gendler, Ruth. *The Book of Qualities*. Berkeley: Turquoise Mountain, 1984.

Gerster, George. *Sahara: Desert of Destiny*. New York: Coward McCann, Inc., 1960.

Gimbutas, Marija. *The Balts*. New York: Frederick A. Praeger, 1963.

_____. *The Language of the Goddess*. San Francisco: Harper & Row, 1989.

Gray, John. *Near Eastern Mythology: Mesopotamia, Syria, Palestine*. New York: Hamlyn Publishing Group, 1969.

Hall, Nor. *The Moon and the Virgin*. New York: Harper & Row, 1981.

Hamilton, Edith. *Mythology: Timeless Tales of Gods and Heroes*. Boston: Little, Brown & Co., 1942.

Hooke, Samuel Henry. *Middle Eastern Mythology: From the Assyrians to the Hebrews*. New York: Penguin, 1963.

Johnson, Buffie. *Lady of the Beasts: Ancient Images of the Goddess and Her Sacred Animals*. San Francisco: Harper & Row, 1988.

Keith, Agnes Newton. *Children of Allah: Between the Sea and the Sahara*. Boston: Little, Brown, & Co., 1965.

MacKenzie, Donald A. *Myths of Pre-Columbian America*. Boston: Longwood Press, 1978.

McCrickard, Janet. *Eclipse of the Sun: An Investigation into Sun and Moon Myths*. Glastonbury, Somerset: Gothic Image Publications, 1990.

Mattoso, Katia M. de Queiros. *To Be a Slave in Brazil*. New Brunswick: Rutgers Univ. Press, 1979.

Mayhall, Mildred P. *The Kiowas*. Norman: Univ. of Oklahoma Press, 1962.

Meldgaard, Jorgen. *Eskimo Sculpture*. New York: Clarkson N. Potter, 1960.

Mellody, Pia. *Facing Codependence*. San Francisco: Harper & Row, 1989.

Miller, Alice. *The Drama of the Gifted Child*. New York: Basic, 1983.

_____. *For Your Own Good*. New York: Farrar, Straus, 1983.

_____. *Thou Shalt Not Be Aware*. New York: New American Library, 1986.

Monaghan, Patricia. *O Mother Sun! A New View of the Cosmic Feminine*. Freedom, CA: The Crossing Press, 1994.

Morrison, Boone, and Malcolm Naea Chun. *Images of the Hula*. Volcano, HI: Summit Press, 1983.

Mukerjee, Radhakamal. *The Culture and Art of India*. New York: Praeger, 1959.

Pagels, Elaine. *The Gnostic Gospels*. New York: Random House, 1979.

Roberts, Jane. *The Nature of Personal Reality*. Englewood Cliffs, NJ: Prentice-Hall, 1974.

Schaef, Anne Wilson. *Women's Reality.* San Francisco: Harper & Row, 1982.

Schafer, Edward H. *The Divine Woman: Dragon Ladies and Rain Maidens.* San Francisco: North Point Press, 1980.

Shuttle, Penelope, and Peter Redgrove. *The Wise Wound: Menstruation and Everywoman.* New York: Grove Press, 1988.

Sjoo, Monica, and Barbara Mor. *The Great Cosmic Mother: Rediscovering the Religion of the Earth.* San Francisco: Harper & Row, 1987.

Spretnak, Charlene. *The Spiritual Dimension of Green Politics.* Santa Fe: Bear & Co., 1986.

Starhawk. *Dreaming the Dark.* Boston: Beacon Press, 1989.

_____. *The Spiral Dance.* San Francisco: Harper & Row, 1989.

_____. *Truth or Dare.* San Francisco: Harper & Row, 1987.

Stone, Merlin. *Ancient Mirrors of Womanhood.* Boston: Beacon Press, [1979] 1984.

_____. *When God Was a Woman.* New York: Dial Press, 1976.

Sturluson, Snorri. *Prose Edda.* Translated by Jean I. Young. Cambridge: Bowes and Bowes, 1954.

Swimme, Brian. *The Universe Is a Green Dragon.* Santa Fe: Bear & Co., 1984.

Teish, Luisah. *Jambalaya.* San Francisco: Harper & Row, 1985.

von Franz, Marie-Louise. *Problems of the Feminine in Fairytales.* Dallas: Spring Publications, 1972.

_____. *Shadow and Evil in Fairytales.* Dallas: Spring Publications, 1974.

Walker, Alice. *The Temple of My Familiar.* New York: Harcourt, Brace, Jovanovich, 1989.

Walker, Barbara. *The Crone.* San Francisco: Harper & Row, 1985.

_____. *The Skeptical Feminist.* San Francisco: Harper & Row, 1987.

_____. *The Woman's Encyclopedia of Myths and Secrets.* San Francisco: Harper & Row, 1983.

Weigle, Marta. *Spiders and Spinsters: Women & Mythology.* Albuquerque: Univ. of New Mexico Press, 1982.

Wunder, John R. *The Kiowa.* New York: Chelsea House Publishers, 1989.

Yarmolinsky, Avrahm, ed. *Two Centuries of Russian Verse: An Anthology.* New York: Random House, 1966.

Zimmer, Heinrich. *Myths and Symbols in Indian Art and Culture.* Princeton, NJ: Princeton Univ. Press, 1946.